Alex Rae

Jaika

Children of Regar

Editors: Brenda Wright and
B. L. Henderson

Cover design © 2016 by P. W. Bledsoe,
Sherrie Sanchez and Casey Moore

Boat Tiger Books

Paperback ISBN 978-0-9984633-1-5

Kindle ISBN 978-0-9984633-0-8

FREE BONUS CHAPTER

Visit my website

https://alexraebooks.wordpress.com/

to explore other books in the *Children of Regar* series and to receive a

FREE BONUS CHAPTER

Table of Contents

Prophecy

In the most ancient of days, our people did not live as we do now. War and fear did not control our lives. There was peace in our land and all Regarians lived as one. The Tal and the Breen, the Benjee and the Sesti.

Each sect would send their wisest men to council at new phase of the red moon. They would pray to the life giver, Gelquin, and seek wisdom. They would resolve disputes and plan for our tomorrows.

There was order. And there was peace.

But in those ancient days there arose a prophet who could see tomorrow. A reader of dreams, a seer of visions. He brought with him a prophecy that would forever change our world. He brought a warning about the future.

The moons of Regar
Shall future see
A dark-eyed princess
Come to thee

Born of power
Raised of ruin
Fed by prophets
Her nature turned

Her heart to Regar
Peace will bring
But serve destruction
To the lesser king

Now Regar was already a world of peace, so no one believed his tale of destruction. And a dark-eyed princess — this could never be. Regar bred no dark-eyed children of any species.

To convince the people of his prophecy's truth, the prophet undertook the impossible. He produced a SolStone. A blue, Azura gem spoken of only in legends. A stone with unimaginable power. The power to heal. The power to destroy.

He used the SolStone to change the people's hearts, performing magic and mysteries. Healing the injured and giving comfort to the broken. Soon all believed in him and not the life giver. Their allegiance was to the prophet, the prophecy, and the majestic SolStone. Their prayers stopped and their hearts grew cold.

It is said that the prophet once followed the life giver, Gelquin. That his heart was once pure as any Regarian, but his heart was turned. The power of the SolStone proved to be too strong even for the prophet.

War broke out among the sects. Crafters of metal set their hands to making weapons. Sculptors fashioned rock walls and high towers. Each man turning against the other. Breen against Sesti, Tal against Benjee. Each leader longing to control the SolStone and fearing the destruction revealed in the prophecy. The destruction promised to the lesser king.

In time, the prophet disappeared, the SolStone was lost, but the wars remained. There were no dark eyes then. Blue and amber, gold and green, but never dark... never dark.

So the people watched for the dark-eyed one, the one to restore peace to Regar. Still clinging to the words of the prophet, they watched...

and waited...

and fought...

Hide and Seek

Jaika stared at Ree through the vines trying desperately to be still. She was tired of watching the wingarings buzzing and glowing atop the leaves and her finger itched. Why wasn't he looking for her? That's why they came to the forest. At least that's what he had told her. Come and play he had said. The red Manchura trees are blooming. The sky is clear. The wingarings are glowing. It's a perfect day for hiding and chasing. But now instead of searching, he was talking with two boys from the Benjee sect. Talking in quiet, serious, grown-up voices that meant their conversation would go on forever. The longer he talked, the harder it was for Jaika to be still.

They were too far away from her hiding spot to hear their words, but she could see them well enough. The tallest boy was a little older than Ree. Eleven, maybe twelve. He made his hands into fists when he talked, thumping them against his leg. The other boy was a little younger, maybe. It was hard to be sure. But they weren't from Palon, that was clear enough.

They didn't have blue eyes, tanned skin, or rumpled sand-colored hair like Ree. In fact, they didn't look at all like regular people. Not like the people in her city anyway. Not like her or Ree. Oh, they had two arms and legs, two eyes and ears. Their bodies curved in the same shapes, but they were different. The golden skinned, amber eyed Benjee; shining people Ree called them. Like they had been dipped in the shimmering metal her father used for armor. Their hair sleek and white. Not at all like Ree's. Not at all like hers. Besides, everyone knew it was forbidden to talk to *them*. The laws decreed it. There had been too many battles. She could almost hear her father preaching the possible dangers.

But Jaika knew she would never tell on Ree. They seemed nice enough and if Ree thought it was important to talk to them then it must be, whatever the law said. Ree was almost ten turns old, and he was the wisest boy she had ever known. Much wiser than her, especially since she was only six turns.

Soon he would stop talking and remember he was supposed to find her. He would come to the viney patch first. He always did. It was her favorite place to hide. The leaves were wide and almost black. Jaika's coarse, dark hair and eyes blended perfectly with the leaves, and beneath the vines she could hear the river – the distant rushing and churning. The river that flowed beneath the bridge. A slivering old shell of a bridge that no one would ever use to cross the river. Crumbling, splintering, wooden planks jutting out into the water just far enough for climbing but not for crossing over. The bridge where Ree could no longer try to catch her. The end of the game. The safe spot.

She was certain Ree already knew where to find her. He kept looking in her direction every few seconds. She was trying so hard to keep the leaves still but her knees were getting tired and she was starting to get thirsty. Even the delicate antics of the wingarings had lost their appeal.

A pale blue boy of the Tal sect appeared from behind a tree, just beyond the boys. Jaika watched him flex his wings as he walked toward the group. He didn't look happy and his voice was louder than it should have been.

"Please don't tell them I came." A voice whispered behind Jaika. It was not the Tal boy at all.

"Who's there?" Jaika asked the bushes. "Are you a bad person?"

"Of course not." A slender blue girl, not much older than Jaika, waved from the bushes. "I had to see you. You are Jaika, right?" She wiggled her wings in excitement.

Jaika did her best to look stern. "It is dangerous to be here, young lady." She hoped she sounded just like her father. "How do you know my name? Is that your brother?" Jaika scooted closer. She had never seen a Tal up close.

"Yes, that's him, my brother, he told me all about you. You are Jaika. You will save the world."

Jaika forgot to be stern. "I can't save the world. I am too little." She studied her visitor's pale blue skin and darker blue eyes. There were feathery blue lines along her face just in front of her ears. Her wings pulled tight behind her body making them difficult to see.

"Not now, silly. You will save us when you are big, like my brother."

Jaika didn't think she wanted to save the world. That should be Ree's job, or maybe her father's.

"I brought you a gift." The girl smiled, then handed Jaika a bracelet made of string and beads. "Please, will you take it?"

Jaika took the bracelet from her tiny hands. "Thank you," was all she could think to say. "Can you really fly?"

The girl giggled. "Of course I can."

"Can you carry me?" Jaika's eyes grew wide at the thought of flying.

"Maybe my brother could." She looked past Jaika at the boys standing among the trees. "I have to go. He will be mad if he sees me."

"I won't tell," Jaika grinned.

"I know you won't... thank you for saving us." The girl disappeared into the leaves.

She must be confused thought Jaika, turning her eyes to Ree and the others. The oldest Benjee boy raised his arm in farewell and Jaika squinched her eyes shut trying her best to look invisible. Ree would come find her now, and she would never tell him about her secret friend. She slipped the bracelet into her pocket, vowing again to keep it a secret.

She could already hear Ree's footsteps coming closer. The leaves crunching beneath his boots. Jaika peeked just a little. Just enough to see Ree's shaggy blonde head moving past.

"Jaika!" He called, walking in random circles, perfectly aware of the wiggly, white-dressed girl in the vines just out of reach. "Oh Jaika, where are you?" The dark vines concealed her face but the white dress, that was another matter.

Jaika clenched her teeth to stifle an anxious giggle.

"I cannot find her anywhere! She is too smart for me." Ree turned his face to hide his amusement from the viney patch. "All free! All free!" He called with a laugh.

Jaika was off in a flash. Exploding out of the vines to shoot across the leafy ground. Before Ree could even turn around, she had passed him heading toward the water, toward the river, toward the wooden planked bridge and safety.

Weaving between the red Manchura trees, jumping over rocks, Jaika flew across the forest ground. She could hear Ree close behind.

"I'm going to get you – you little sneak."

Jaika laughed as she ran. The river's roar carrying her giggles away. One, two, three steps and she was on the bridge, collapsing to her knees, drinking her air.

"I win again," she called in-between breaths.

She heard Ree's lumbering steps as he climbed the bridge.

"You win. Now it's time to go home Jaika. No more searching." Ree's face had grown cloudy.

Jaika whirled to her feet, glaring at her friend. "No! No! No!" she shouted, jumping up and down with each word. Her voice almost a whisper against the rushing waters below the wooden bridge.

The river was no more than ten men across, she had heard her father say, but it held the strength of a thousand.

"No! No!" Jaika shouted again, jumping harder atop the bridge.

"Yes! Yes! Yes!" Ree chanted, joining in the dance. The clouds gone from his eyes. They never lasted long when Jaika was with him.

Jaika squealed in delight, giggling and jumping. "No! No! No!"

"Yes, yes, yes," Ree countered, stomping and pounding against the wooden planks. The bridge thudded with the weight of their bodies, groaning with the strain.

Jaika felt the wood give way even before she heard the splintering crack of the bridge. Her body quivered and floated before it dropped.

In a frenzied panic Jaika clawed at Ree, watching him slip through the boards and feeling her own body fall. Her fingers raked the boy's shirt, sliding along his body to finally catch his boot. Her head whip-cracked backwards as Ree stopped their fall. He clung to the broken boards, only his head above the bridge. Jaika dangled from his left leg, her fingers digging deep into the flesh above his boots.

"Ree!" she shrieked, but her cry was lost in the roar of the water. Icy froth licked at her bare ankles and slicked her dress to her knees.

She tried to look up at Ree, to scream his name again, but her face stayed buried against his leg. "1, 2, 3...," she counted in her mind. "4, 5, 6..." Ree said to count when you're afraid. The numbers make you not afraid. "7, 8, 9...," she whispered. "Don't let go. Hold on."

Ree shook as the jagged boards tore into his arms

and chest. He knew if he let go they would both drown. He might survive the rapids but Jaika would never see the other side alive.

Ree twisted his body to face the smooth planking still intact. Each plank was only one hand's width and there were cracks between them. Cracks big enough for his fingers. Planks with cracks, almost a ladder in disguise.

His arms trembled with the strain. Jaika must weigh as much as a saktar, he thought, digging his fingers between the boards. With clenched jaw, he pulled. His chest slipping above the first plank. He reached forward with his left hand to the next plank. His fingers wedging between the cracks. Ree could feel the splinters scraping his hands and the wood tearing into his shirt, burning into his chest. But worst of all, he could feel Jaika slipping.

Right hand, left hand, he climbed, pulling himself across the planking until only his legs hung below the bridge. With one swing his right knee was safe. His body twisting to raise his leg free. Now pushing with one knee as well as climbing with his hands, he kept moving forward. His right leg screaming as if it would snap into, but he kept moving, wiggling, twisting in ways he didn't know his body could bend, grabbing at his ankle, reaching for Jaika. His fingers wrapped around her tiny wrists, burrowing deep into her flesh. With one painful jerk, he pulled her upper body onto the splintering bridge. Jaika hooked her fingers into his pants and climbed. Like she would a Manchura tree, she climbed until both their bodies shivered and collapsed side by side atop the bridge.

Ree stared skyward watching the sun, too exhausted to move any further.

"Ree," Jaika whispered beside his ear. "Ree!" she shrieked, sitting straight up.

Wild-eyed, Jaika stared at her hands. Blood stained her fingers and palms. She stared at Ree's shirt and the jagged, diagonal tear from his chest to his waist. She stared at the dark red smear across his shirt and down his pants.

"Hush, Jaika," the boy commanded, forcing his hand to reach for hers. His chest burned and his arms felt useless.

But she couldn't take her eyes away. They were drawn to the open wound torn across Ree's body. The wound caused by the collapsing bridge. The awful, horrible price he had paid saving her life.

Jaika bit her lip and tried not to cry. Ree hated it when she cried, but she couldn't stop. No matter how hard she tried, the tears escaped. Fiery, body shaking tears.

But Ree didn't seem to mind. He just held her hand and waited, watching the quiet blue of the sky, feeling weak but deliciously glad they were alive.

The Hero

Jaika's dark eyes beamed as she chattered and danced about the playroom deep in the belly of Merith's castle. Her tiny body bounced from spot to spot sending her black curls tumbling around her face and shoulders.

"Tell the tale, Ree!" she cried. "I want to hear it again. Tell the tale."

Inita, the caregiver, watched patiently from the corner of the stone room, swaying gently in her wooden rocker, watching Ree smile at his friend dancing and weaving about the room. No one else could draw Ree out like Jaika, make him smile, make him strong. He was never quite the same boy when they were apart, as though a piece of him were missing.

The two children had been inseparable since Jaika had been placed in Inita's care. Jaika's father simply had no time for a small child. His wife's death had left Jaika without guidance, so Inita had taken the job of caregiver. After all, she considered it an honor to care for the king's daughter, Merith's daughter, Princess Jaika. Ree's father, Keshar, was just as busy as the king, but the Captain of the Guard would never have admitted his boy might need a caregiver, even for a moment. But it was safer if Ree stayed with Jaika and Inita even if it was unofficial.

Ree leaned his head against the gray stone. Sitting down he seemed quite tall for a boy ten turns old. His body lean and tan with his chest wrapped in white bandages. The gash across his chest had not been deep enough to damage any vital organs, but it would leave a menacing scar. Of course, according to Ree, it was all in a day's work for the son of the Captain of the Guard.

He raised his arm and ran his fingers through his tousled, blonde hair. "No more stories, Jaika. I've told it five times already."

Inita laughed and scooted her rocker away from the wall giving her Azura pendant a hypnotic swing. An odd, triangular stone, jagged and pale. Not a particularly pretty necklace, but it had been a gift from Merith. A gift from the king himself. Inita would have worn a broken twig around her neck if it would please her king.

She was quite frail for a woman so young. Delicate as glass. Her tunic style dress hanging from her narrow shoulders. Her thin body and pale skin matching the soft sadness in her eyes. The wars had taken their toll on many families, and Inita's was no exception.

"Ree saved me," Jaika sang, still dancing about the room. Her feet following the circular patterns on the heavy rug that covered the cold, stone floor.

The playroom was empty save for a few chairs and woolen rug. Jaika's doll rested in the corner near Ree's bow and tattered story book. Beside Inita's rocker a pale, green glass held the flickering light of a captured wingaring inside. Its random song sent ripples along the walls of its prison.

When it was dangerous outside, her father would let others into the castle. There would be so many people. Everyone trying to eat and find a place to sleep.

She remembered hearing her father talk about the balance between keeping the soldiers fed and strong and still feeding all the people. If the people die, then nothing else would matter. She thought she understood, but she wasn't sure. There was always food to eat. She didn't remember ever being hungry. But her father said it was not that way for everyone. So when her father had to take care of the people, he would send his precious Jaika with Ree into the playroom, into the lower part of the castle, to make sure they would be safe.

Inita glanced down at Jaika's pet wingaring and at the heating unit just beyond. The white crystal burned low in the heater and would need to be replaced soon. One crystal would run the heater for almost a month, but they were not as easy to come by as they used to be. Renegades had destroyed many of the mines, and the crystals that powered most of the kingdom were in short supply. With limited fuel and the constant danger of attack the children were safer here, with her.

Jaika's soft tunic and sweater were little protection against the chill, but she never noticed. She just kept dancing. "Ree saved me from the water," chanted Jaika. "He saved me from the water."

"One more time?" pleaded Ree. "If I tell it one more time will you be happy?"

"One more time," mocked Jaika, obviously pleased with her success.

Ree rarely said no to her. In the six turns of her life, he could remember only twice.

"One more time. But, only if you promise to rest when I am finished...Picari."

Ree knew that nickname annoyed Jaika to her very bones. A blue-brown mark on her neck resembled a Picari bird, her father had said. A tiny bird that flew wildly in all directions, often without purpose or plan. Jaika did not want to be a Picari bird, so she promised to be still and positioned herself directly in front of her friend. She crossed her legs and rested her chin in her hands, ready for the long story. Her eyes steady on Ree's face, watching his every move. Someday she would be as brave as he was, or at least she hoped so.

#

She was never really sure how long it took to reach help. Jaika remembered running out of the trees, past the shops with rainbow colored tents flapping in the afternoon breeze. The customers wandering across the dirt covered ground staring at the wild-eyed girl. The soldier that whisked her into his arms and listened to her out-of-breath story, gasping and describing Ree and the awful blood.

She remembered all of these things, in an instant, as if they had happened all at once. But Ree was safe now. The blood was gone, and that was all that mattered.

"We were playing by the river," Ree sighed. "Jaika was hiding from me. She is a good hider."

Jaika raised her proud chin. This was high praise indeed, even though the Regarian forest provided many hiding places. The red leafed Manchura trees were always in bloom, and a broad patch of spotted vine was always easy to find.

"I could not find her, so I yelled 'free.' Jaika was behind a tree." Ree rolled his eyes and sighed again. He had only pretended not to see her. Staying hidden and quiet at the same time was almost impossible for his tiny companion.

She clapped her hands in delight. "I was safe. I got to the bridge. Ree couldn't catch me." She almost sang the words.

"That's right," smiled Ree. "So I went out on the

bridge with Jaika, and it broke."

"Ree got hurt. The bridge cut Ree," affirmed Jaika, reaching toward the bandages across his chest.

Ree winced, remembering the sharp pain inflicted by the jagged boards of the old, wooden bridge. His leg still burned from Jaika's tight grip where she had buried her fingers into his skin to keep from crashing into the rushing water below. It had taken every ounce of his strength to climb back onto the bridge with Jaika holding to his leg.

"Enough stories," cooed Inita. "Time for everyone to be in bed. Her soft, blue eyes illuminated her simple face. The same pale blue of the Azura stone pendant that dangled around her neck. But then, everyone in Palon had blue eyes. Everyone... except Jaika.

#

"Open the gate! Open the gate!" Voices echoed across the stone of Merith's castle. From the high walls the watchman could see a single rider coming in from the sandy wasteland. Tired hoof beats kicking up the dust as a saktar carried its owner home. A powerful, black saktar with fur covered feet. A saktar that could only belong to the Captain of the Guard.

Once safe inside the castle walls, the broad-shouldered Captain dismounted and removed his helmet.

Sweat tangled his dark hair and beard. Dirt streaked his face and clothes. He wore the same gray, tuniced uniform as any soldier. The blood-red star on his right shoulder was the only sign of his special rank.

Keshar had ridden hard and without sleep for two days to reach King Merith. It had been a difficult journey for a man his age. Ha, he thought to himself. It would have been a rough ride for a man half his age. At 42 he was still young enough to take on any soldier in his ranks, but maybe not just now.

A young boy bowed to the Captain and led away the black stallion to be cared for while two soldiers escorted Keshar straight to the King. Through the outer wooden doors and down a silvery, rock hallway, they led the way directly to Merith. These walls were nothing like the gray stone of the sublevels where the children played. Here, the sunlight could reach most of the rock and change its color from gray to white, leaving only the shadowy places untouched.

Shields and swords decorated the hallway walls. Many broken or damaged. Prized souvenirs of a past battle, a victory won, a life lost. Pink, green, and a few of the rare yellow glowers grew from pots along the hallway casting rainbows of light along the white rock. The glow from their leaves lit the castle as fine as any crystal.

Keshar couldn't help but remember the days when clear crystal light had bathed these hallways. When glowers had been used only for children or celebrations. The colors from the glowers were pleasing enough, but they served as a constant reminder to Keshar that his people, Regar's people, lived in danger.

In the throne room, bright red and yellow carpets covered the middle of a shimmering stone floor. They depicted dazzling, geometric designs of happier days. Six man-sized paintings of great battles and mounted soldiers covered the side walls. Three on each. A throne made out of the same silvery, white rock in the walls and floor waited atop three stone steps at the end of the room.

So did King Merith.

Lean and dark haired, he sat stiff backed with his hands folded in his lap. His eyes blue as any Regarian's. His face clean shaven and strong. His thoughts tangled in a fishnet of despair. He didn't want to hear Keshar's report but there was no other way...

"I have news your majesty," proclaimed Keshar with a deep bow before the king.

Merith moved his head in solemn acknowledgment.

"Kaleus's army is growing. He has amassed at least 200 men. Some are afoot, some on beasts." Keshar paused a moment to catch his breath then did his best to continue in spite of his exhaustion. "He has allied with the ruler of Devant. He means to take your daughter and destroy Palon in the process. He knows..."

Merith closed his eyes to hide his fear from the Captain. He had been planning for this moment since Jaika's birth. Since he had seen those beautiful, dark eyes. Merith had never really believed his Jaika was the dark-eyed one predicted in the prophecy, but it didn't matter what he believed, only what his enemies believed. If they knew of her eyes, then...

"I had hoped she would be older before...I lost her," he whispered cautiously, wishing the words were not true.

Merith had become king at the young age of seventeen, but fifteen turns as ruler had taught him a great deal. Kaleus had already killed his wife, and he would not allow anything to happen to his daughter. Prophecy or not, she must be protected.

Merith's cape floated behind him as he descended the steps from the throne. He wore no crown, but the Palon star graced the front of his silver tunic. A crown was unnecessary. There was no mistaking his authority. Even the air around him felt invincible.

Merith placed a firm hand on his friend's shoulder. The king was not a big man and stood a good hand's width shorter than the Captain, but there was no question as to their rank. Merith was king. Keshar would follow him anywhere. They shared a trust that only comes with time and trials. Merith trusted Keshar with his life, and his precious Jaika.

The king drew a sigh of strength. "Are you strong enough to make the journey, my friend?"

Merith's quivering voice took Keshar by surprise. He had never seen such fear in the young king. They had faced enemies far greater than the army that threatened them now and Merith had never once slowed in hesitation.

The Captain straightened his back and drew a deep breath. He could deny his king nothing. "I will find the strength, Sire. We will deliver Jaika safely to the Guardians."

The Greatest Warrior

Galimar stood alone on the night sand. A giant of a man. His warrior's strength hidden beneath a Guardian's cloak. Its hood drawn low over his face – always covering his face. He grew his sandy colored hair long and a beard to hide most of the scars, but those around his left eye pulled and distorted his flesh making it look a little like dried mud. Only the hood covered every mark. Clothing could hide his face and the burns that ran the length of his arms, but nothing could change them. Nothing could ever take them away or the memories of how they came to be.

He stood just outside the stone building he had called home for the past two turns. Beyond the city of Palon where the fertile land dissolved into the barren desert. Farther than any castle walls or merchant's tent. Far from Merith and those he loved.

This tiny stone building had been a place of hiding

for the once great Galimar. A place of solitude and healing. A place of study. Here he had been taught the ways of the Guardians, their beliefs, their knowledge. As a soldier, he had no use for such knowledge, but then, he was no longer a soldier.

These rock walls and dirt floors were most often silent and empty. A barren place with little furniture and even fewer conveniences. He had spent most of these last two turns alone, visited and schooled only by the other Palon Guardians, Oberon and Eron, and of course, King Merith. But tonight was different. Tonight Oberon and Eron had brought news of a most disturbing nature.

Tonight, everything would change.

Tonight, Merith was bringing Jaika.

Galimar watched the stars and thought of his friend, little Jaika. She always loved the lights of the sky. She could find the saktar and the Breen shapes in the stars, but the red moon was her favorite. He wondered if it was still her favorite. In two turns many things had changed.

His pulse quickened as he thought of the changes still to come and the danger the darkness held. Tonight, Merith would bring Jaika. Merith would trust him with his daughter again, trust him to protect her. Just as he had two turns ago, before that day in the market...

Suddenly his chest felt hollow and he tried not to think about it. He just studied the stars and the silhouetted city and the lights of Merith's castle, straining to see any warning that troops approached. He listened as much as watched. And he waited. Patience had become a close friend of the Guardian Galimar.

"Are you sure he's coming?" Galimar whispered into the darkness, aware that Oberon watched from the window of the stone house. Oberon, leader of the Guardians.

"I still think this is a poor hiding place for Merith's daughter... but yes... he said he would come tonight."

Galimar turned to stare at Oberon, looking down into his anxious face. Dark and thin, silhouetted against the glower light behind him. He appeared like a sorcerer out of the rock house, moving from the window to the doorway.

Like Galimar, he wore the dark robe of a Guardian but without a hood. He had no scars to hide. His face was chiseled in a handsome line with steel blue eyes and olive skin. His dark hair and close cut beard granted him a sculptured appearance, as if his wiry body had been artificially cut from stone. Galimar often wondered if Oberon's heart had been cut from that same stone.

"He knows they search for Jaika," Oberon continued. "Merith must come tonight."

"Tonight?" Galimar repeated. His voice gentle with hope that there was some mistake.

"My message was from King Merith, personally,"

cautioned Oberon. Galimar's complacency drove him to madness, and who was he to question.

"Do you really think the Princess will be safe here?" A youthful voice questioned from somewhere behind Oberon. Eron had been listening from inside the stone building.

"Safer than in the castle if the raiders come." Galimar answered, turning his gaze back to the city.

Oberon licked his lips. "I think he means will she be safe with you?"

Galimar's heart winced with the tenderness of an old wound. Even here, away from the city, among people he trusted, he was never allowed to forget his failures.

Beneath the hooded robe, no one saw the pain, but Oberon knew he had hit the mark.

"He will not come alone," Galimar reasoned quietly. "Jaika will have soldiers to protect her... and there is always Keshar." Though two turns had passed since he had visited the castle, he placed his eternal faith in the Captain of the Guard. He would succeed where Galimar had failed.

Eron, the youngest Guardian, pushed his way past Oberon to join Galimar on the endless sand. The boy was every bit as tall as the warrior but his cloak hung formless around his tapered frame making him look small beside the mountainous Galimar. His hood crumpled around his shoulders exposing unruly curls and an overpowering naivety.

The boy sputtered with nervous laughter. "Merith's guards have always protected us," he said. "Why should this night be any different?"

Galimar sighed with forbearance, "I wish I possessed your unwavering faith, Eron." He spoke with only a backward glance, his eyes never leaving the city's shadow. "Have you already forgotten Kaleus's last raid on the city?"

"No. But Merith stopped his army, and he will prevail again." Eron made his announcement with great pride, filled with the confidence that comes only with youth and inexperience.

Oberon moved back inside the stone house, enjoying Eron's nervous chatter. Kaleus's army was on the move. They had seen the dust clouds just before night fall. Fear was thick in the air. Even the courageous Galimar could not deny the strain.

"Whatever happens," commanded Galimar, "we must protect the princess."

Eron shifted his feet, unaccustomed to Galimar's forceful tone.

Oberon only smiled.

#

A heavy darkness blanketed the seven figures that followed Merith out of the city. Cloaked figures riding in close formation. Jaika shared a saddle with her father. Keshar and Inita followed in their shadow with three of the king's most trusted men just behind. The main army was left to protect the city of Palon, to stop Kaleus's raiders if the need arose. Tonight they must fight without their king.

Merith pulled his robe around his daughter to keep her warm. His saktar moving in gentle rhythm beneath their weight in a slow, deliberate pace. The king was in no hurry. The time for good-byes would come soon enough.

The travelers picked their way through the scattered houses and inns that dotted the edge of the kingdom. Merchants' tents with the flaps tied down. Boarded up shanties that served food and drink to the most unsavory of Regarians. The wisest of citizens built their homes close to the protection of the castle walls, but there were always those willing to risk danger if it provided a profit. Here the law was lenient, the soldiers were few if any, but the risk of Kaleus's raiders was unavoidable.

Jaika clung to the slick saddle and buried her hands in her father's woolen cape, thankful for the safety of his arms. She possessed an adventurer's heart but it was much easier to be brave when she was with her father.

She had never been in this part of the city but she

knew she didn't like it. The buildings looked tired and afraid. Even the people hid from the night. Jaika watched Regar's two moons as she rode and thought of the pictures in the stars. The pictures that could guide you home Gali had said. The red moon was always changing, the yellow moon sometimes vanishing all together, but the stars were forever. She closed her eyes a moment and wished he was here. He knew the answer to every question. Even when no one else had time, Gali would listen, and he would know the answer. He would have told her where they were going tonight. He would have told her...

#

Oberon was the first to hear their saktars. He stood at the doorway watching the tiny band of travelers make their way toward the stone house, knowing things would be different after this night. Jaika would stay with the three of them until the danger passed, if it ever passed. He didn't exactly relish the idea of raising a child and the idea of working constantly with Galimar was even more distasteful, but his duty to Merith must come first.

As the travelers arrived, he watched Keshar slip from his saktar and then lift Inita from her mount. He would recognize that pale girl in any light. Merith stayed in his saddle, staring at the stone house as though he was considering a change in plan. His saktar shifted his weight nervously on the sand.

"Be brave, my little Picari," he whispered into Jaika's ear.

Oberon heard the great sigh that escaped the king before he lowered his daughter to the ground and dismounted. Their hands linked as they entered the stone house. Merith's heavy robes whirling with every step, surrounding Jaika's tiny frame. Inita and Keshar followed only a few steps behind. The three gray tuniced soldiers remained mounted and battle ready.

Galimar waited in the shadows of the tiny house. His shoulders tight with the dread of what must follow.

"Welcome, your Majesty," announced Oberon with a formal bow. His voice matched the deep black of his hair and the steel of his eyes.

Merith merely nodded and scanned the room with impatience until his eyes found Galimar. "I am relieved to see that you are safe. Kaleus has not discovered you."

"Are you expecting him?" Eron stammered, fidgeting with the tasseled belt on his robe, trying not to look terrified.

"It is inevitable." Merith looked down to smile at his daughter. "That is why we are here."

Jaika stared up into her father's face, her dark eyes bursting with adoration. She didn't understand what was happening or why they were here. She just knew it was important. At least it was important to her father and that made it important to her.

She wanted to make him proud, more than anything she wanted to make him proud. So she held her chin as bravely as she could and stood beside him even though her heart beat wildly in her throat.

"My Lord," Galimar spoke as he moved out from the shadows to face the king. He lowered his head in formal acknowledgment, his face still covered. Merith returned his limited bow as did Keshar and Inita.

Oberon cleared his throat with disapproval. He found their reverence for Galimar to be quite nauseating. How could they still hold him in such high regard? His carelessness had cost Jaika her mother. How could anyone forgive that?

"Galimar," Merith drew on his fading resolve. "Are you ready?"

Oberon passed a questioning glance toward Merith. He was the leader. Why would Merith question Galimar?

At the sound of her friend's name, Jaika's heart jumped. This man hiding under the cape, was he really Galimar? She let go of her father's hand and moved closer.

"As your messenger instructed, my King. But, surely there must be another way?" Galimar's dislike for the situation was clear.

As Galimar spoke, Jaika wove her hand through the folds of his cloak. She slipped her hand to the back of his knee. It had been almost two turns since she had heard his melodious voice or felt his mighty arms scoop her from the ground, but she remembered.

"Gali?" Jaika whispered. A little afraid that beneath the robes her friend would not remember her.

Jaika saw her father's hand reach out for her.

"Yes, my Jaika," Galimar assured. "I am here." The sadness in his voice was inescapable.

Oberon didn't think he could take much more of this tender reunion, so he answered for Galimar. "Yes, Merith, we are ready to protect Jaika."

Galimar nodded, slipping away from Jaika and motioning for the others to follow.

Only three rooms divided the small house and Galimar led the way to his bedroom. A tiny cot for sleeping, one chair, and a thin shelf of tattered books.

Unfinished canvases leaned against the far walls. One painting showed a great battle with gleaming swords. Hundreds of multi-colored flowers covered another. Still more paintings were of the Krill, creatures with tentacle like arms that swayed as they walked. Jaika saw the winged Breen and Omahr. She knew Galimar had seen all of these creatures. He had told her about the dangers and the lives lost, but she didn't know he could paint them. She would definitely have to tell Ree about this place.

Galimar removed three books from the middle shelf of the bookcase and took out a wooden box. It was nothing special to behold. Just a worn wooden box no bigger than the books that had protected it, but Galimar held it as though it were more precious than the king's crown.

He slipped his hand inside his robe and raised a key that hung from a chord around his neck. The key fit into the front of the box, and it opened.

Jaika stood on tiptoe to see what was inside.

A mixture of anger and confusion hovered over the Guardian's leader. Oberon raised his open hands toward Merith. His body stiffened, and his eyes narrowed. "What is happening?" demanded Oberon. "Why have you kept such secrets?" He looked at the box as if it would burn his hands if he touched it.

Galimar stared at Merith, waiting to see if he would explain. He had kept the king's plan a secret for two turns and he had hated every second.

Merith did not acknowledge Oberon's questions, so Galimar continued. He dug his fingers into the box and removed a blue glossy disk no bigger than Jaika's hand. An amulet of stone... Azura blue... a SolStone.

Oberon looked at Eron for support but he was lost in amazement at the unfolding events.

Galimar held the amulet suspended from a silver

chain. His sleeve slid to his elbow and Jaika could see the red scars that marred his arm and hand. Her eyes grew wide and her heart beat faster than she ever thought possible.

Pictures and letters were etched deep into the sleek surface of the stone. Only one edge revealed any signs of imperfection. One edge had a triangular gash tearing into its side as though the stone had been dropped or broken.

The longer Galimar held it, the brighter it became until it glowed with the blue-white sparkle of the stars.

Jaika reached out her tiny hand to touch its shinning beauty. Galimar quickly covered her fingers with his giant's hand. "Not yet my little one."

Oberon's face was as hard as the amulet itself. "What is this?" His anger sliced into each word.

"A SolStone," Galimar explained. His gentle words enraging Oberon even further.

"The SolStone is only a legend," Oberon contended, fighting to hold his temper in front of the king. "Only a legend. There is no such thing... where did you get that?" His face reddened with every word.

"I gave it to him." Merith stated, leaving no room for questions. "I have been entrusted with its secrets. I will do with it as I see fit."

Oberon took a step backward and lowered his eyes. "Yes, of course." But he didn't understand at all and his anger burned at Merith's slight.

Galimar held the stone toward Oberon. "I was given the SolStone to study because I lived alone and could work unobserved. For two turns I have practiced with the SolStone, learning to use its powers as best I could, trying to find a way to protect Jaika."

At the sound of her name the tiny princess squeezed her father's hand. She was glad Gali had a magic necklace but she wasn't sure what it had to do with her.

Oberon clenched his teeth. Galimar was trying to appease him but he would have none of his excuses. Merith had always shown favoritism to this man. This man who should be in prison or worse. This man who had failed his king and brought only pain to his family. Why had Merith trusted Galimar with the SolStone – with such power? Why not him? Oberon, leader of the Guardians. His knowledge was greater than Galimar's. He deserved the SolStone, he had earned it. Why had Merith betrayed him?

Eron was without words. He just stood back against the doorway, watching the men in the room. Merith and Galimar guarded their emotions, kept their feelings in check, but Oberon was afraid. Angry and afraid. Somehow the sight of Oberon losing control made him feel incredibly small, so Eron just did nothing.

"Now what happens?" Oberon flung his cloak over his shoulder to reveal a creamy white tunic and pants. "Now we destroy Kaleus and his army? We use the SolStone to destroy all our enemies?"

"It's not that easy," Galimar shook his head. "Its powers must be used for creation, for good, never for destruction."

"Then what are we going to *create*?" Oberon growled, his eyes smoldering. "You and Merith obviously have a plan. A plan that doesn't include me."

"Not a plan Oberon, a place." Galimar held the amulet high in the air.

"It's time, Galimar," Merith commanded. His apprehension buried beneath the duties he wore as the king, and as Jaika's father.

The Guardian Galimar nodded and laid the amulet in the palm of his hand. His great fingers closing around it, covering it completely.

Jaika drew her body close to her father's leg, waiting for something horrible to happen. She peered at Keshar and Inita from behind her father's cape. Her caregiver seemed as confused as everyone else. Her face white against the rock walls. And her necklace — the blue Azura pendant was glowing. The same blue-white color as the necklace Galimar had taken from the box. The princess pointed with a trembling finger but no one paid any attention.

Galimar squeezed the amulet until his fingers turned as white at Inita's face. A quivering sigh escaped the cloaked man and the air began to move.

The air behind him shimmered and danced, turning the same blue-white as the amulet. The light thickened and quieted, making a wall of what looked like sticky water.

Galimar relaxed his hand in exhaustion, almost dropping the amulet.

"A doorway," Oberon marveled. "To where?"

"A place where Jaika will be safe," Galimar looked at Oberon even though his friend could not see his eyes. "A place where Kaleus cannot follow."

Oberon did not wish to listen. "I will not be part of this. How can you send this child through...there?" He began to back away from the wall of light.

Merith already understood that there was no coming back from this place but somehow Galimar needed to hear the words. "Are you certain there can be no other solution?" pleaded Galimar.

Merith drew a long, slow breath. He stood firm, never flinching, but Galimar caught the glimmer of hopelessness in his weary eyes. His shoulders did not stand quite as proud as before. "I have considered the options. This is my final decision."

Galimar closed his eyes to escape, just for a moment, what he knew would follow. "Do you remember what I told you?" Galimar inquired of Inita, wishing she were a warrior. "The red stone building. You must find it."

Jaika's caregiver stood as far away from the light as possible, clinging to the gray wall of the house, hiding among the few available shadows.

"I remember," she stammered. "Through the trees, across the smooth stone road to the red rock house, just like you said."

Jaika looked up into her father's face. Sometimes he seemed as tall as any building in the kingdom, and she was awfully glad he was her father and no one else's. She stiffened her shoulders and did her best to look fearless in his shadow. But she wasn't fearless at all. In fact, she was terrified. She had never heard of this magic necklace or the blue, watery wall much less considered walking through it. It would be alright, she told herself. She wasn't sure where they were going but she would be fine as long as her father was beside her.

Merith knelt beside his daughter and pulled her close. His heart felt as if it would burst. "You must go with Inita," he whispered, holding her frightened face in his hands. "You must be brave, beloved. It is the only way to keep you safe." Merith's words were controlled and filled with artificial courage.

"Father?" Jaika hesitated. A sickening lump formed in the pit of her stomach as she realized he wasn't coming with her. Why, she wanted to yell. Why can't you come? Why can't I stay with you?

"This is a great honor," her father said. "You will be the first Regarian child to travel by the SolStone."

With a heavy sigh, she resigned herself to the fact that she was going into the light without her father. It must not be a bad thing or he would never make her go. He loved her and whatever this blue light did it must be very important. She would do whatever he asked of her even if she didn't understand why.

With a mixture of fear and excitement, Jaika stared at the shimmering wall. She didn't understand that Kaleus's raiders had become a full-scale army and that they were coming to Palon. She didn't understand that her world was in terrible danger. She only knew she didn't want to leave her father.

Jaika buried her face against Merith's shoulder.

Inita reached for her courage. She remembered her own family. The family the raiders had destroyed, and she wasn't going to let that happen again. For Jaika's sake, she would be strong. "We have to go now," she explained, pulling herself from the wall, patting the young girls arm.

"I love you," Merith struggled with the words. "Never forget."

"Father," Jaika whispered into his ear. "Will you let my wingaring go when you get home? It's bad luck if it dies, you know. I left it in the playroom."

Merith drew Jaika even closer. He had no strength

to answer.

Inita pulled Jaika from her father's embrace and started to move to the wall of light.

Galimar stopped them. He lifted the SolStone close to Inita's chest. He held it beside her Azura pendant and then brought the two together. They both shared the same blue-white light. Glowing side-by-side, she could see the two had once been one. The jagged, triangular pendant she wore fit the gash in the side of the SolStone.

"The SolStone can find you, wherever you are. That is why I had you wear it. So I could find you, you and Jaika. On Regar or on any other world. I will always be able to find you."

He nodded and moved to let them pass.

Holding the princess close to her side, their hands unbreakably linked, Inita turned toward the light. She never looked back. She knew her courage would fail if she saw the heartache in Merith's eyes. Her king. Her unbreakable, fearless king.

"1, 2, 3..." Jaika counted her steps. "4, 5, 6...7, 8, 9."

And they were gone.

Departure

The light stung Jaika's eyes as she clung to Inita's arm. It took five steps to reach the other side. The princess was disappointed to say the least. She had expected to fly or slide a little. At least there could have been some sparkling lights and colors. But, there was nothing. They simply stepped through the wavering air and they were on the other side.

Inita pulled Jaika close, and they turned to look back toward Merith, but they could not see through the watery wall. And then it was gone. As the doorway vanished so did the blue light in Inita's pendant. It hung around her neck lifeless and dark. The magic gone, just like Regar and all that Jaika loved so well.

All they could see were plain, green trees and bushes. Tall, thick and healthy, but plain none-the-less. There were no flowers, no colors. Not like the trees on Regar that held fruits and blossoms almost every day.

Jaika squeezed Inita's hand and thought of Gali and her father just a few steps away, or maybe even farther than the greater mountains. She wasn't sure any more. She thought of Ree and the stories she could tell him. Maybe...someday...she would see him again and she could tell him everything.

"1, 2, 3...," Jaika whispered, making sure Inita couldn't hear. "4, 5, 6 steps." Steps to somewhere. Somewhere ...

#

Merith nodded slowly to Galimar, watching the light fade from the amulet, watching the watery doorway close and vanish, watching his Jaika disappear forever.

"Merith," Galimar whispered into the heart-wrenching silence.

Merith closed his eyes and waited for the world to end. His wife was gone and now his daughter, so the world as he knew it was over.

"Finish the job," Merith whispered. His face was as lifeless as the amulet in his friend's hand.

"Yes, your majesty," Galimar's body slumped beneath his cloak. He knew Merith did not intend for anyone to follow Jaika.

"We must finish the job." The king turned to

Keshar and Galimar, drawing strength from his followers, his friends.

Galimar laid the cold, stone amulet on the rickety table beside the bed. Then he knelt beside his cot and reached beneath it and removed a narrow, black cloth bag from the shadows. He lifted the bundle into his arms, cradling it as a man might cradle a child. When he stood, the velvety, black fabric slipped to the floor to reveal a broad sword. Silver handled with a blade as wide as a man's hand. Galimar's sword. A warrior's sword.

The guardian then turned toward the table and with mechanical precision raised his sword above his head.

Oberon watched in shock and horror. His eyes wild. His mouth open to scream, to stop Galimar. The word 'no' had barely left his mouth when he heard the metallic splintering of the amulet beneath the blade. He watched the shards spray across the table onto the dirt floor.

In an instant Oberon was on his knees digging the tiny pieces from the ground, cradling them in his hands. Each sliver glowing in his grasp. A pale, sickly blue light flickering and fading fast.

"Why? why?" Oberon murmured as he scraped at the dirt. Over and over the word fell from his lips until it became an angry shout. "Why have you done this?"

Galimar gripped his sword with numb fingers and

walked past the frantic guardian scrambling on the floor. "For Jaika," he answered, pausing a moment beside Merith. "I did it for Jaika."

Merith reached out to touch his friend's arm. He knew the guardian's pain was every bit as great as his own. In losing Jaika, they had both lost a part of their lives.

Oberon glared at the two men in front of him, and in that instant his heart was filled with more hatred than he had ever thought possible. A black hate. The kind of hate that drives men to madness. Merith would pay for what he'd done. Merith and his pet Galimar. They had deceived him, and worse, they had destroyed the SolStone.

As Galimar left the tiny room, Merith looked to Keshar, sharing a look of painfully clear understanding. Keshar pulled a metallic cube from a woolen bag laced to his belt. A crystalline fusure bomb, a butcher box.

The cube fit nicely in his hands, and he turned it over and over, applying pressure to each colored face in sequence, setting the spring driven controls.

Oberon could hold his sanity no longer. "You will not destroy this place!" he shrieked and flung himself at the Captain, driving his hands toward the man's throat and dropping the SolStone fragments he held so dear. Keshar met Oberon's tirade with a strong fist and sent him reeling against the wall. The Captain shrugged off a look of annoyance and continued his work.

Oberon clung to the wall until his vision cleared. He wiped the back of his hand across the tiny trickle of blood that warmed the corner of his mouth. Keshar was a part of all of this, he thought. Merith, Galimar, now Keshar. They were all against him. But that would change. They would be sorry when he controlled the SolStone.

Keeping one eye on Keshar, Oberon knelt to retrieve the fallen pieces of the amulet, knowing soon this whole building would be nothing but rubble.

Keshar completed the arming sequence and laid the bomb on the table. The same table that had held the SolStone steady for Galimar only moments before.

"It's time to go," Keshar commanded, casting his pity toward Oberon. "You have only a few moments."

When the guardian did not stand or even acknowledge his understanding, Keshar left without him, left him alone digging blue stone pieces out of the dust, alone with the pulsating fusure bomb.

Keshar found Merith already mounted and waiting outside the rock house. Galimar and two soldiers waited beside him, each atop their own saktar and anxious to be on their way. Eron stood holding the reins of three fidgeting mounts, looking every bit as frightened as the saktars.

"Where's Oberon?" Eron shouted, the rising wind sweeping his words away.

The Captain shook his head and tried not think about what would happen to the man. "We can't wait for him," he shouted in return.

Eron stifled the sickening worry that covered him, just as his guardian's cloak. He was afraid for Oberon, but he wasn't going back into that building. Not alone.

The saktars tossed their heads and strained against their straps, pulling Eron backward into the sand. Keshar took the reins from Eron. "Get on!" he commanded, holding Eron's mount still while he clambered into the saddle. Then, slipping onto his own saktar.

Merith and the others were already on the move, their saktars carrying them back to Palon, without Jaika or Inita. Keshar and Eron dug in their heels and hurried to catch up.

When Galimar's home exploded, Keshar's only reaction was to duck his head. Stony debris pelted his back and arms. Eron wiped at the blood that oozed down his cheek just under his eye and pressed his body against his saktar's neck, afraid to think of what might have happened to Oberon. Was he buried in the collapsing rock, or simply reduced to dust by Keshar's bomb?

Merith dug his heels into his saktar's side, spurring him forward, toward home. There would be a battle tonight. It may have already started. The night wind would drown any war cries or clashing steel, but he would listen anyway. He hated this world of war. It had cost him so much. A part of him was glad Jaika could travel on to a safe place, a place without war, a place where she might know happiness. But a part of him knew his heart would never be whole again. That losing Jaika was more painful than the wound from any sword. First his wife and now his daughter, gone forever. There would be no others. He would not allow himself the luxury of love ever again.

So he rode, toward Palon, toward the battle, and welcomed his death and the freedom it offered.

Behind the travelers, beyond the remains of the temple, Oberon prodded his saktar into the strong wind. Blood trickled from his mouth and the cuts across his arms. He would carry the scars from this night forever. The scars that Merith caused.

"Move faster you stupid animal!" He drew his hood to cover his face from the wind and stinging sand, then patted a worn pouch tied to the neck straps of his saktar. A pale, blue glow radiated from the top of the open bag.

Arrival

It was night in this world, just like on Regar. But, in this village there were no glowers to guide their way, only misty lights from wooden poles. White lights without color, not like the glowers of Regar. And this place had only one moon in its sky: one pale, white moon. Jaika missed the red moon already.

The trees were bare and the ground looked dead and dry. Small buds along the limbs promised leaves or maybe flowers, but it was barren compared to the Regarian forest. No Manchura red blossoms or black leaved vines. The air was cold and stale.

Jaika watched for any signs of life, but they seemed completely alone. I hope Father remembers my wingaring, she thought. Whispering "1,2,3..." just in case she might feel afraid.

Inita and Jaika plodded slowly through the trees toward the dull, red stone building that Galimar had described. She could see its outline in the distance. There were other buildings around it, and Jaika could just make out the movement of people. The thought of meeting strangers made her tighten her grip on Inita's hand.

As they walked, Jaika looked down to see the hard, dirt ground give way to the smooth gray rock of a pathway then change again into a rough, black road. Inita pulled her close as a loud wagon with wheels and blinding lights whizzed by in front of them. Jaika had never seen a wagon move so quickly and without a saktar to pull it. It roared louder than a Bartok and looked just as dangerous.

They clung to each other as they crossed the empty street. Inita kept looking around to make sure none of those strange machines came back.

Steep steps led to the building's front entrance. Letters above the doorway on a once white banner read "Mission House." Jaika could only wonder at the meaning. People lined the sides of the steps like weary soldiers in rank. Dirty, strong smelling people with the aroma of medicine. The nasty kind that everyone hates to drink. Jaika did not like the dim lights and rock pathways, but she followed Inita obediently. In fact, she stayed as close to her friend as possible reminding herself that her father would never have sent them to a dangerous place.

"...4,5,6," she whispered, not wanting Inita to hear.

The double doors into the building had windows covered with heavy bars. Jaika could see in through those frosty, sweat-soaked windows as they climbed the steps. Inside there were people everywhere.

The warm inviting smell of food covered them both as they stepped inside. Men and women milled around the room like bugs, so no one noticed the two new arrivals. The room was filled with six long tables full of hungry people. A dozen or more stood in a line along the back wall waiting to be served across a metallic counter. The room felt warm and inviting despite the strange mix of aromas.

A roly-poly woman with graying hair pulled up in a fat bun waddled over toward Jaika and Inita. "Are you two hungry tonight?" She smiled with every inch of her chubby face.

"A naw kee bakarou," Inita spoke the words very slowly. Her answer brought a strange look to the other woman's face.

"Oh," she laughed and jiggled all over, "foreigners. I wonder where you're from. Oh it don't matter nun. I can talk plenty for both of you. Howard! Come and give me a hand."

A frail, little man looked up from the line of people in the back. "In a minute, Mrs. Box," he muttered. His head was covered with a stiff cloth that stuck out in all directions around his face. Jaika thought it might be a tool to catch rain water.

"Oh, never mind," she smirked. "I'll do it myself."

Mrs. Box walked over to a soft box by the door and pulled out two worn, pink blankets. Quickly, she waddled back to drape one over Inita's shoulders. With an overdone sweeping motion, she indicated that they should follow her. "Come...with...me," she said. Her words long and slow as if that would make them easier to understand.

Inita nodded, and she led the way to a long wooden table lined with people busy stuffing their faces with food. One or two people glanced up at their arrival, but no one stopped eating.

Jaika stared at the strangers. Many had dark skin and their eyes were many different colors. Some had light skin like Jaika, but everyone looked very strange. One young man had hair that grew in sharp spikes on his head and a silver ring in his nose. Jaika had never seen such a variety of creatures and all eating together, side by side, with no fighting. On Regar, each species stayed away from the others. They would risk great battles to keep strangers out of their land.

Jaika sat down in one of the metal chairs, while Mrs. Box waddled through the tables and people to the counters across the back wall. Soon she returned with a red tray that held two steaming bowls of soup and several pieces of yellow bread. Jaika was not really hungry, but the sweet aroma of the beef stew was too tempting.

Jaika wondered why all of these people were here.

Why weren't they with their families or in their homes? Inita must have been thinking the same thing because she hugged Jaika close and whispered not to worry.

They nibbled at their meals trying to decide what each ingredient might be. When they had finished, Mrs. Box removed their plates and led them past the tables to a separate room. Here there was a great sea of metal cots and lumpy mattresses strewn across the floor. Three people slept along one wall, but most of the beds were empty.

Mrs. Box pointed to two of the newer looking cots and Inita nodded pushing back the distaste she felt for her surroundings, wearing her mask of bravery. Inita tried to say thank you with pieces of Regarian phrases and some hand motions. Somehow, Mrs. Box understood and answered with a flabby faced grin. Then she waddled away shouting to Howard that she needed his help.

Inita sat down on the cot and pulled Jaika up into her lap gently rocking the tiny girl as she sang a Regarian lullaby. Jaika thought of Ree and her father and wondered if they missed her. Ree wouldn't have anyone to play with now and who would take care of him while Inita was here with Jaika? The warm tears burned her eyes. She hoped they wouldn't forget her wingaring.

Mrs. Harmon

"Ugghhh," Jaika moaned as she strained to move. The muscles in her body cried out in pain with every motion. Her head felt as if it would burst at any moment. A white light misted above her, while a mechanical hum stood just out of reach. The hum was broken at regular intervals by an irritating beep. Each beep matched the beating of Jaika's heart.

Someone pressed a cool rag across her burning forehead.

"Do not be afraid, little one," a gentle whisper came from beside the bed. Jaika did not recognize the voice, but her words were kind and the rag soothed her hot face.

The lights in the white room were painfully bright, and it was difficult to see. At first, Jaika could only squint at the shapes around her, but her vision was slowly returning. She could just make out the woman beside the bed. Her skin and hair were dark. Jaika had never seen anyone with such beautiful skin. And her eyes, they were warm and dark, just like Jaika's.

She wanted to watch the woman, but her eyes were heavy. She could not stay awake any longer. So once again, she was lost in the lights.

The next time Jaika awakened, she was totally alone. The bright lights still shone in her face, but the kind lady with the cool rag had vanished.

"Inita?" Jaika's uncertain words echoed inside the empty room.

The door swung open, and a woman dressed in cool, green clothes peered into Jaika's room.

"You're awake," she smiled. "Are you hungry?"

Jaika pulled the covers up to her neck and stared at the woman. She gripped the hand railing that edged the hospital bed.

"An a Inita?" Jaika whispered. Where was her care giver? Why wasn't she here?

A sad expression flooded the nurse's green eyes. "Oh, sweetheart," she hesitated. How could she ever explain that the fever had just been too strong? Telling someone about a death was hard enough, but this poor child didn't even understand English.

Jaika continued her wide-eyed stare, not knowing

what else to do.

"I know just what you need," the nurse called as she disappeared.

She returned in only a moment with a tray full of goodies. "This is milk," she explained. "The sandwich has ham on it, and of course you will want potato chips." She smiled and point to a small cup. "And this is ice cream. It's chocolate."

Jaika was afraid, but she was also very hungry. The nurse laid the tray on a rolling table that slid across the top of Jaika's bed.

"Hungry?" The nurse asked again, as she handed Jaika part of the sandwich.

Cautiously, Jaika took the tiniest bite from the sandwich. Whatever this was, it was delicious, and soon she was devouring everything on the plate. She felt as if she hadn't eaten in days. And in fact, she hadn't. If Jaika had been able to understand the nurse's words, she would have known that four days had passed since she walked through the shining wall into this new world.

When the tray was empty, Jaika collapsed back onto the bed, exhausted again. Eating had taken every bit of her strength. The kind nurse sat by her bed until Jaika slept again.

The next morning, voices interrupted Jaika's sleep. The words were strange, but she recognized that concerned tone. Inita used that same tone when Jaika was not being careful.

She was still in the bright room, but this time the dark-skinned lady was back. She smiled when she saw Jaika sit up.

"Good morning, little one," the same sweet voice she had used when Jaika was sick.

"Mrs. Harmon, I really do not think you should take her home. You are too old to take care of a child."

"Let's be careful who we call old," Mrs. Harmon raised her eyebrows at the nurse. "Besides, she has nowhere else to go. She can't even speak English."

"The police are trying..."

"The police have not been any help. They cannot even identify her language." Mrs. Harmon sat down on the edge of Jaika's bed. "She needs me." And in her heart, way down deep, Mattie Harmon needed Jaika too. Age was fast becoming the cruelest of wardens, diminishing her necessity in this wide world – taking away the work she loved.

Mrs. Harmon's compassion touched Jaika's heart. Even though she did not understand the meaning of her words, she could hear the concern. Jaika studied Mrs. Harmon for a moment, wondering if she had any children of her own. With cautious movements, she crawled out from under the covers and edged her way toward Mrs. Harmon. Slowly she reached out to touch her hand. Her dark skin felt warm and a little wrinkled just like her grandmother's hand had felt the only time they had met. Jaika dove into her arms and snuggled close. There could be no mistake. Whoever this woman was, she was a friend, and Jaika needed a friend.

That afternoon, Mrs. Harmon brought Jaika some clean, new clothes. She washed her face and brushed her ragged curls and tried to explain that Inita had not been able to overcome the fever. She had died the night they came to the hospital; their very first night in the city. Jaika would watch and listen closely, but she could not understand.

Then Mrs. Harmon pulled a long chain from her jacket pocket and slipped it over Jaika's head. Inita's Azura pendant dropped against her clean, white shirt. Jaika's hand trembled as she caught hold of the pendant. Her chest felt empty and hollow as though her heart had died.

"Inita?" She choked on her name. Inita loved this necklace. She would never take it off. Unless...Jaika closed her eyes and counted...1, 2, 3. It wasn't helping...4, 5, 6. Inita was gone. Something horrible had happened. 7, 8, 9... There could never be enough numbers. Inita wasn't coming back.

Mrs. Harmon held her until the tears stopped.

New Home

Jaika tried to be brave as Mrs. Harmon led the way from the hospital room and down the hall to the main entrance. Several nurses stopped to wave good-bye. They all seemed to be wearing the same clothes, and Jaika wondered what their tribe might be called. She listened to Mrs. Harmon's footsteps echoing along the hallway, and the mechanical shush of the tall, glass doors opening magically as they drew near.

She tried so hard not to cry, but the silent tears ran down Jaika's cheeks anyway. Hand in hand they walked toward row after row of those loud machines. Those machines with wheels that had terrified her and Inita the night they arrived.

Jaika glanced over her shoulder at the giant building behind them. The sides were smooth and shiny, a little bit like her father's castle. She hoped he would come and see her soon. She wanted to tell him about

Inita and her new friend. Maybe he would bring Ree too.

They walked in-between the now-silent machines, and Jaika shrank back afraid to touch them.

"You've never ridden in a car before, have you little one?" Mrs. Harmon's voice was soothing as she patted the young girl's arm. "I will protect you, Jaika."

Jaika's eyes grew wide at the sound of her name. No one from this world had spoken it before. Somehow it made it a little easier to be brave. How could she know that Mrs. Harmon had listened to Inita repeating her name, calling for Jaika over and over as the fever took her life.

Mrs. Harmon led Jaika beside a two-door Chevrolet. She pounded on the green door several times and then let Jaika have a turn. A few whacks and she knew there was nothing to fear.

"Carrr." Mrs. Harmon pronounced the word slowly.

"Car." Jaika caught on immediately. "Car!" she yelled, "Car, car, car!"

Mrs. Harmon opened the door, but Jaika would not go in. It took several demonstrations before Jaika would follow. Soon they both were buckled in and ready for the road.

Mrs. Harmon held up the key ring and said "Key." Thirty-five years as a school teacher would come in handy. Jaika had a great deal to learn.

"Key." Jaika was proud. "Key...car." She pronounced each syllable with care.

As soon as the key turned, the car came to life. Jaika screamed and put her hands over her ears.

"This is going to take some time," sighed Mrs. Harmon.

She backed out of the parking place and headed toward the street. Jaika was quickly caught up in the new sights of Earth and completely forgot to be afraid. She chattered in broken Regarian, pointing at buildings and people. Whenever possible, Mrs. Harmon provided the English names...house, light, tree. Jaika was already learning. She stuck her arm outside the window to feel the air pushing against her hand. She was traveling faster than anyone she had ever seen. Ree would be so jealous.

Soon they arrived at Mrs. Harmon's home. Mattie, as Jaika would soon come to call her, lived in a tiny, shingled house. The sides were a buttery yellow with robin's egg blue on the trim and shutters. Deep green plants grew in terra-cotta pots along the short walkway that curved up to meet the porch. A ladder-back rocking chair waited beside the doorway.

Mattie used her key and led Jaika inside. The rooms were as small and simply furnished as the outside. Most rooms were visible from the entrance. The front room held a pale flowered couch and a slim high backed chair. Two short stools and a table with chairs filled up the kitchen.

Jaika wandered from room to room, anxious to see everything. The furnishings were worn and the lace curtains that covered most of the windows had yellowed with age. But in Jaika's eyes, everything was brand new. She had never seen lace curtains or a couch or a headboard, so old or new did not mean a thing to her. But clean, that she understood. Everything was spotless. It was a peaceful, orderly house. Everything was in its place. The smell of soap mingled in the air with the morning's perfume. But the most amazing sight in the whole house was the books.

Every room held books. Jaika had never seen so many.

"I used to teach children to read. I was...and I guess I still am, a teacher." Mattie tried to explain.

Jaika marveled at the shelves filled with books. This woman must be richer than any king. Surely no one on Regar owned so many books. Books were a luxury that many people could not afford. Valuable time was spent making weapons, not hand writing books. Most Regarians focused on their combat practice or marksmanship. There was simply no time for books, only war.

Ssscritch...ssscratch...Jaika turned wide-eyed back toward the kitchen. Surely Mattie could hear that sound, but she didn't seem worried at all.

On her tiptoes, Jaika followed the sound. Mrs. Harmon only watched as she made her way into the kitchen to stare at the back door. The scratching grew in intensity, as though some wild beast was trying to get in. Jaika kept glancing back and forth from Mattie to the door and back to Mattie.

"That's just my Sam," Mrs. Harmon laughed, moving into the kitchen and pulling open the back door.

Jaika jumped back as a tiny creature raced into the kitchen and around the table several times. He made yapping noises as he sniffed at her shoes and the wonderful new smells.

"Saaaam," Mattie made the word sound like it was a mile long.

Jaika slid to her knees as Sam caught her nose with a lick. "Sam," Jaika giggled, "Sam." It was hard to be afraid with so many new things to see.

Mattie smiled. Sam liked her. That was a good thing. It would have been hard to choose between the two of them if he had not. She laughed to herself and motioned for Jaika to follow her. Together they headed toward the back of the house and its two bedrooms. The hallway ended with two matching doors. Jaika stood in the hallway turning her head side to side, looking directly into each room.

The room on the left was smaller and held a smaller bed with very little else. White plank walls surrounded a dresser, a mirror, and that little bed. Jaika could not take her eyes off of that bed. The blanket on top of the bed was white with big pink polka dots – dots the size of plates. It looked like nothing else in the house. Mattie walked over to the bed and gently slid her hand across the fabric, stopping to swirl her finger around a dot.

"It was a gift," she whispered. Jaika thought she could see a tear tugging at Ms. Harmon's eye. "He said I needed a little chaos in my life." She smiled. "After he was gone, I just couldn't bring myself to give it up."

Jaika wondered why Mattie would keep something that made her sad. Even if it was really fun to look at.

"This will be your bed, my dear. You can sleep in here for as long as you like."

Jaika didn't understand, but she knew those were good words she was hearing, words that were welcoming her into this home. She sat on the edge of the bed watching Sam watching her. She could hear animals singing in the flowerless trees outside the house. In the distance, children giggled and chattered – somewhere down the street – in another house.

Mattie's house was much smaller than her father's white stone castle. There were no glowers or wingarings, but this place had a Mattie and a Sam. And, there did not seem to be any hiding places for protection if the soldiers came. Maybe there were no soldiers. Maybe her father was right. Maybe she would be okay... but her heart still hurt anyway.

Rosie

Jaika stood in front of the double glass doors that led into Emmanuel Elementary School. 'Six months,' Mattie had said. 'It has been six months since you came to me. That's long enough to be lazy.'

Jaika had no idea what six months meant, but if Mattie said it had been long enough – then it had been long enough. And so here they were, in front of Emmanuel Elementary School.

School, Jaika thought, there must a word just like that in every language? A word that means a place to go to learn new things. As far as Jaika was concerned, almost everything here was a new thing, so it didn't really matter where they were.

Mattie held her hand as they walked into the building. A nice lady with long hair gave Mattie a stack of papers to write on, and they walked over to a table in the corner to sit down. As Mattie wrote, Jaika watched other children, accompanied by an adult, go to the same table. Each time, she tried to figure out if the grownup was their mother or father or a guardian. Sometimes the grownups didn't look anything at all like the child they were with. Their eyes or their skin were often a very different color. She thought of Regar and the blue-eyed people she missed. Sometimes it was hard to remember their faces. At night she would practice remembering, but it was getting harder every day.

Mattie sat beside her and started making marks on the paper. She would write something and then look up at Jaika and shake her head. "I wish I knew your story," Mattie said, looking at Jaika's questioning eyes.

Jaika knew she was supposed to have an answer, but she wasn't sure how to tell Mattie she had walked through a shimmering wall of light to get here.

Soon Mattie stood and motioned for Jaika to follow. They gave the papers back to the lady with the long hair. And that's when Jaika saw her – the girl she would come to know as Rosie. She stood in her guardian's shadow. A tall man with the coldest eyes Jaika had ever seen. She had dark hair and a dress covered with tiny red flowers. Her waist was tied with a wide, red ribbon. But somewhere beneath the polished flowers and ribbons, beat the heart of a wild animal. Jaika was sure everyone in the room could hear it pounding.

This wild girl peeked sideways at Jaika from under her lashes; her gaze wavering from the ground to Jaika and back to the ground again, trying to use her best camouflage techniques. Rosie finally met her gaze, eye to eye, straight on, and that's when Jaika knew they would become friends.

Rosie's guardian spoke to the lady at the table and then turned to see the girls. Jaika was sure he was a guardian or a soldier. His eyes told of battle. She had seen that look before. After the soldiers have gone, after the weapons are still, after the bodies have been burned, the people left behind all shared the same lifeless look as Rosie's guardian — faces hiding unspeakable secrets. Each set of eyes reliving something that could never be unseen.

Jaika now knew that this planet had war, just like Regar. The tall man had seen it; maybe Rosie too. Maybe there were no gray tunics or swords, but there was battle here nonetheless. Jaika did not feel safe anymore. "One, two, three," she counted the seconds, watching Rosie and her guardian exit through the tall, glass doors. "Five, six, seven," she would have to be brave...braver than she had ever been before. "Eight, nine, ten," she missed Ree. But her father had a plan, a plan for her and for Ree and for his city. There must be a plan. Jaika kept counting as she took Mattie's hand. When they left the school, Jaika knew that tomorrow would be different. Tomorrow she would begin learning how to live on her own.

Dream

Sunlight dripped like honey through the branches of the Manchura trees — skyscraper trees that surrounded Jaika on every side. She closed her eyes and let the sunlight wash over her skin, raising her face to the sky, drinking in every ounce of light that filtered through the trees...red Manchura trees. Trees that grew only on Regar. Their perfumed blossoms fluttered with the wind's caresses sending bits of white fluff floating through the sunlit air to land on the dark leaves of Viney Patch and creeping yellow Sica that snaked atop the grass and around the base of the trees.

Everything was perfect. The breeze, the sunlight, the trees...and the water. Jaika could hear the river in the distance, in front of her somewhere, beyond the trees, churning, white, frothy water.

"Jaika," a voice whispered.

She looked behind her, sideways and back, but there was no one there. It had certainly sounded like a voice she thought. Maybe it was just the water's echo or her imagination. Jaika drew a deep breath and listened hard.

"Jaika," he called again. A man's voice. A friend's voice.

She heard it clearly this time, reaching out to her through the trees. A voice she knew from somewhere.

Jaika could not resist his call. Her feet moved in his direction, drawn by his voice. Completely spellbound by the shushing of the water and the tenderness in the man's voice, she walked. One step at a time, her bare feet slipping along the grass, moving her closer and closer to the rushing water... and his voice. She had to find this man who called her. She had to find her friend. It was important to find him, though she couldn't think just why.

"Jaika!" the voice called again. His voice stronger this time, more urgent.

She walked more quickly now, gathering up her nightgown so it wouldn't catch on the bushes. The voice had stopped but the water still churned and bubbled, growing louder with every moment, every step, closer, closer... Her heart jumped high into her chest, pounding with as much strength as the water.

"Jaika!" the voice screamed, fearful, anguished,

desperately calling.

Jaika couldn't stand it any longer. She ran. She had to run. The voice, her friend, he needed her. Through the trees she flew, through endless corridors of trees. Her feet carried her past Viney Patch and Creeping Sica. The bushes tearing at her gown, shredding it to fringe around her ankles. Broken twigs and dry grass slicing into her feet.

Then the trees were gone. Patches of grass and sandy rocks covered the ground, and Jaika was no longer running. Her body stood stiff and frozen as if she had hit a brick wall. She could see the river, boiling, swirling white. A rumbling train of a river that shook her body with its roar.

She stood at its edge, feeling the icy spray sting her face and arms, facing the water and the bridge. A narrow, splintering, poor-excuse for a bridge that fought continuously against the water, braving the assault of every wave. The voice came from that bridge. That thin black railing of a bridge that crossed the entire river.

At first her feet would not obey her will to move. They stuck fast in the sand. "1, 2, 3...," she counted, planning her steps to the bridge.

One step, then two, her feet reluctantly complied. Up the steps of the bridge she climbed to the first level plank. It wobbled with her steps. The railings teetered with a rollercoaster jerk. The planks were cracked and broken, some missing all together. Jaika tiptoed across them as if she walked on glass. The bridge grew longer as she walked, stretching out before her eyes, endless.

"Jaika!" a new voice called from behind her, almost lost in the river's roar. "Jaika!" a deep, rumbling voice.

She turned to see a man standing on the river's shore, tall, strong, handsome. He was dressed in gray with a blood-red cape flying in the wind behind him. His tunic bore a red star and his head a golden crown. Jaika could feel his eyes on her, pulling her away from the river and its dangers.

"Jaika!" the brave, young king called, but she could not go back.

She wanted to go back, to fall into his arms where she would be safe, but the bridge vanished behind her with every step. Plank after plank evaporated, leaving only the river in its place. So instead, she held on. Her knuckles white around the bridge's railing, jerking her hands in crack-the-whip fashion.

"Help me!" she screamed, reaching toward the king. If he could just reach her, she would be safe.

He stood helpless on the water's edge. Nothing between him and Jaika but the water.

"Jaika!" screamed another voice — the first voice. The reason she had come to this horrible bridge. She had almost forgotten the sound.

"Jaika!" the voice trembled across the bridge.

She turned away from the king to see a young boy. He was standing on the bridge. His chest was bloody. A ragged wound slashed from his neck to his stomach. Blood oozed from the gash, running down his chest and onto his black pants.

Then, the bridge collapsed beneath her. Every plank shattered into tiny pieces falling into the river below and taking Jaika with it. She fell. Forever, she fell. She could feel the spray of the water and see the sky above her, but she could not stop falling. Then her arm jerked sideways. Something grabbed her arm. Digging into her flesh and pulling her sideways. The boy... the boy on the bridge. The water was below, but Jaika hung by her arm above it. The boy held her high above the water. She could see his deep blue eyes and the blood that ran along his arm.

Jaika gasped and screamed. She screamed with every muscle in her tiny body. The water..., the roar..., the scream...

"Jaika!" But this time, it was Mattie. "Wake up child. You are dreaming."

Mattie's arms surrounded her as the boy let go. Jaika opened her eyes wide and remembered. She remembered Ree on the bridge — her father on the shore — the world she would never see again. Her tears came as fiercely as the water had raged. She buried her face against Mattie's chest and cried. She cried for the boy and for her father. She cried for Inita and the wall of light and the white stone castle and the wingaring. She cried until she could cry no more. As the tears quieted, Mattie climbed into bed beside her. They spent the rest of the night huddled in Jaika's twin bed.

When morning came, they shared a quiet breakfast. Even Sam could feel the worry and stayed under the table to be close. This was not the first bad dream for Jaika, and both of them knew there would be more. Once, Mattie had taken her to meet with a nice man at the hospital who wanted to hear all about her dreams. Jaika did not have the words to tell him about her father and the wall of light. So Mattie did not take her back. They were all nice people trying to do nice thinks for her, but the only one who could make it right was her father. She would wait as long as necessary for him to come. She would get stronger and braver and wait for him to come.

After breakfast, Mattie took her back to the large brick building with the double glass doors. "Emmanuel Elementary School," Jaika pronounced.

The lady with the long hair was there, and she reassured Mrs. Harmon that everything would be alright. Jaika didn't know if she really believed that.

Eventually, she led them down a long hallway – a wonderful hallway painted in yellows and blues. Each door was a different color, and the walls were covered in drawings. Not heavy tapestries like in her father's home, but silly, misshapen pictures like Ree used to draw. Beyond each door she could hear children talking, even laughing sometimes. And there were caregivers too, inside the rooms with the children. Some looked sleepy or bored, but no one looked scared or worried.

A loud warning sound filled the building, and suddenly there were children walking in lines down the hallway. Some were very quiet and serious while others chattered and skipped, quickly catching the warnings of a caregiver. Like Mattie, many of them had beautiful, coffee colored skin. One had fiery red hair, while some had hair so short it looked as if they had none at all. One boy had injured his legs, so he traveled about in a chair with wheels. But, most importantly, many had dark eyes. There were green and blue just like on Regar, but in this world Jaika was not the only one with dark eyes.

The lady with the long hair reached out her hand to Jaika. With a nod of approval from Mattie, they both walked inside one of the rooms. This one had a red door.

The caregiver at the front smiled and introduced herself as Mrs. Rodriguez. All the ladies she had met had that funny word 'misses' in their name. Jaika wondered if it meant bossy or someone who knows everything. Mrs. Rodriguez had short, curly hair and sounded different than Mattie when she talked. Maybe because she was so young, she spoke a different language. Jaika could only understand bits and pieces anyway.

Mrs. Rodriguez showed Jaika where to sit and how to find the paper and pencils. She showed her where she could hang her sweater and find a tissue. And, along the side of the room, she motioned to three bookshelves filled with books. Jaika didn't say a word. She just walked over to the shelves, picked up a tall book of pictures, and sat down on a squishy, yellow pillow.

Mrs. Rodriguez smiled. "I think we are going to get along quite well."

In a few minutes, the other children came back into the room, and Mrs. Harmon waved a sneaky goodbye. There were no shiny skinned people here, no one with wings or scales, but here there was a Rosie. Jaika's heart jumped when she saw Rosie come into the room. She was swinging her arms in stiff, marching fashion. Every three or four steps she would count. 'Hup 2, 3, 4.' Jaika decided she would ask about this Hup person. Today, there were no ribbons or dresses. She wore green pants with brown spots, a black T-shirt, and boots.

Rosie walked right up to Jaika and saluted. "You are the girl I saw when my dad signed me up for school."

Jaika nodded and tried to remember the word for spots. "Your pants?" she questioned.

"These are camo. You know? Camouflage?" She seemed surprised that Jaika didn't know what they were. "They are like my dad's. He was in the army. I'm gonna be too... someday."

Jaika had no idea what the army was or why they wore spotted pants, but it must be a good thing if Rosie liked it.

"You can come and sit with me," she continued. "You're new, and I can take care of you."

Jaika followed Rosie over to four student desks that faced each other to make a square. Three of the desks had a name tag taped to the corner with a student's name written in bold black letters – Rosie, Nick, and Javon.

Rosie pointed to one of the desks. "That used to be Javon's, but he's gone." She lowered her voice to a whisper. "Nobody knows where... but he isn't coming back."

Jaika swallowed hard. Maybe Rosie was teasing, but she couldn't be sure. Jaika would take extra care not to make Mrs. Rodriguez angry. Nick eventually joined them. A thin, wise looking boy with glasses. A pale, blonde, frail looking child with wise, knowing eyes that could explain any secret.

So they all sat together in the four corner desks: Rosie, Jaika, Nick, and the empty chair. Jaika watched to see what to do next. Jaika watched Mrs. Rodriguez and Rosie and this Nick person who had joined them. In fact, for most of that day all Jaika did was watch...and listen. Mattie had worked hard to prepare her for school, but she could not teach her everything. Jaika knew her letters and colors and many of her numbers. She could write 25 different words and spell them correctly...most of the time. But there were so many other things Mattie had skipped.

Jaika did learn that Mrs. Rodriguez was a teacher not a caregiver. She learned that students who are last in the lunch line do not get much time to eat. And she learned that an hour can feel like an entire day while a teacher is talking.

Rosie taught her how to say 'estupida' and 'loco' in Spanish and to bounce a ball while standing in one of four squares. Nick showed her how to whistle through the hole where his front tooth should have been. He also taught her a word that made Mrs. Rodriguez's face turn red. Jaika decided not to tell Mattie about that word. It must be one of those words only soldiers can use. Her father had warned her about such things.

At the end of the day, Jaika drug her backpack and followed the class to the front exit. Mattie was standing patiently by the double glass doors holding a bag of chicken nuggets. Jaika had never been so hungry in her whole life. Ree would have liked chicken nuggets.

Jack

The days flew by, and Jaika grew a little taller and a great deal smarter thanks to Mattie and Rosie. At school they did everything together. Jaika and Rosie were inseparable. They sat together, ate lunch together, and even sometimes rode the bus together. They learned English and taught each other their own languages. Jaika learned some Spanish and Rosie learned a few words of Regarian even though she would never be able to speak it to anyone. Rosie never doubted Jaika's story about the wall of light and her home in another place. As far as they both knew, Regar might simply be in another country. After all, in elementary school, it is easy to believe in everything.

Nick was often a tag-a-long, whistling his words through his teeth. "Yesss Mrsssss Rodriguezzzzz," he would say, sending the whole class into an uproar of giggles. It was hard to decide if his lisp was a performance or a happy accident.

Mattie took Jaika to school almost every day. The building was close to their home, so on sunny days, they would walk. Sometimes even Sam would come with them. Mattie tied him to a rope, so he would not run away. Sam slept in Jaika's bed most nights. He would lick her face on the nights that the dream returned, which wasn't that often any more. The water and Ree and her father were getting harder and harder to remember. Their faces seemed far away sometimes. Mattie would say that our hearts work that way. When we lose someone we love, we must learn to love someone else. Jaika knew she was Mattie's someone else. She had peeked at the photographs hidden in the table drawer next to Mattie's bed. Two men in uniform — smiling, happy, living forever in those tattered pictures. One was much older than the other. Jaika wasn't sure who they were, but Mattie had loved them — that was the important part. So if it was true, and Jaika needed to love someone else to fill the hole in her heart — Mattie, and Sam, would be her someone else.

Javon never did come back to claim his desk, so Jaika kept the seat beside Rosie and Nick. Everything was going smoothly — new friends, new school, new information...

and then...

there was Jack.

Jack arrived exactly eight weeks and three days

after school began. This was his third school for the year, but the students didn't know that. No one in the class really understood that when a student gets in enough trouble, he can be expelled from school forever. In fact, Jack had been expelled seventeen times.

Because he had missed so many days of school, he was almost two years older than everyone in Jaika's class and at least a foot taller. His towering height quickly earned him the nickname of Jack the Giant Killer. His words made it clear that he hated everyone in the room, just like Jack had hated the giant at the top of that beanstalk, or so the story goes. And when you hate everyone, there is only one possible outcome. Everyone will begin to hate you right back.

Jack could throw a rock ten feet and hit a kid in the back without anyone of importance, namely a teacher, ever seeing him. He could thump your ear twice before you even knew he was behind you. He could hit harder and reach higher than any other student in the class. It was easy to believe that if a giant should ever come into their classroom, Jack would be able to take him down.

Mrs. Rodriguez always walked beside him in line, but he still managed to find trouble. Jaika and Rosie made it a point to stay out of his way, sometimes walking to the other side of the classroom to avoid the slightest eye contact. Maybe it was an illusion, but Mrs. Rodriguez seemed to grow much older after Jack's arrival. The wrinkles at the corners of her eyes deepened, and her bright smile shrunk into a tiny nod of approval.

The days grew shorter and colder until the school closed for Thanksgiving. What a wonderful holiday! Jaika could hardly believe that school would close for a whole week just so everyone could eat food — special food — lots of food. She couldn't think of anything better than that. Even in her father's house, food could be scarce. The night meal might be bread and broth... sometimes just bread. There were always lots of green leafy foods to eat, but who wanted those. If the soldiers had time to hunt, a warm piece of meat might be a welcome addition. Jaika always wondered what the other children ate, in other houses, in other cities.

In Mattie's house, today, there was no doubt that the food would be special. The house positively glowed. The scent of warm turkey, buttery breads, and something chocolate floated throughout the rooms. Even the bathroom smelled delicious. Jaika couldn't know that this was the first family holiday for Mattie in twelve years. She couldn't know that every wonderful smell was baking just for her.

As the day progressed, Jaika learned where the special table covers were kept and how to warm them in the drying machine to take away the wrinkles. She helped Mattie take out the special dishes one piece at a time and position them in alignment on the table cover leaving room for a basket in the center with fresh cut flowers. Cloth napkins and candles, shiny spoons and forks, everything had its place. A food holiday was truly a wonderful thing!

When they finally sat down to eat, Jaika was exhausted just from salivating. She quickly decided that turkey must be like coffee, it just didn't smell quite like it tasted. But the buttered rolls were exactly what she expected. Excluding dessert, the highlight of the meal was the macaroni covered with thick creamy cheese sauce. Jaika ate two bowls and begged to save some for later. If there was any left on Monday, maybe she could sneak some to Rosie in her backpack without it getting squished under her notebook of course. But the chocolate pie was not going anywhere but into Jaika's stomach.

The following morning, Mattie took Jaika back to the dull, red brick building to see Mrs. Box, the roly-poly woman with graying hair. The same brick building where Jaika had spent her first night here in this new world. The same brick building where she had lost Inita.

But, this time Jaika was not a visitor. This time, Jaika and Mattie were here to work. They spent the morning unpacking bags of plastic silverware and napkins. They peeled potatoes, stirred gravy, and cooked until the whole room smelled buttery warm.

Once the people started arriving, Jaika worked behind the counter with Mattie and six other people whose names she didn't remember. She couldn't reach high enough to serve food, but she could hand out napkins and forks. She could refill the empty straw holder and deliver extra rolls, warm rolls, good rolls, but not like Mattie's rolls.

Most of the people smelled like the street and wore clothes that were too big or torn. One man had a shiny new coat to keep him warm, and he sparkled among the crowd of dirty faces. But no matter how worn or weary, everyone was happy. The room was full of thank-yous and grateful hearts.

Jaika thought of the day she had followed Inita through the watery wall of light. The fear and confusion of that time seemed so far away. This dull building had been a place of safety on that day, and it made her wonder just how far each of these people had traveled. She searched the crowd for signs of Regar, but mostly, she just tried to be kind. If any of these people had just come to this world, Jaika wanted them to remember her and this place with a smile.

Thursday

The week went by in the blink of an eye, and it was time for school to start again. It was good to see Rosie and Nick, and Mrs. Rodriguez looking like a brand-new person. She had a new haircut with long sweeping bangs and shiny pink polish on her nails. Jack was absent for the first three days and most of the class found themselves hoping he would never return. But on Thursday... it happened... Jack came back.

Rosie scooted her chair a little closer to Jaika's when Jack walked in the room. His eyes were dark and hard and ready for a fight. Jaika didn't think he had eaten chocolate pie or buttery rolls during the holidays. Maybe he didn't even have a family.

He took his seat at the front of the room. Rosie thought she heard Mrs. Rodriguez whimper just a little. No one said anything for at least a whole minute. The silence pressed against the walls, and then the teacher continued her lesson as though nothing had changed. Jaika tried to listen. There would be a spelling test on Friday and a math practice to take home, and why was Jack so angry? She watched him sulking at the front of the room. He might cry at any minute, she thought.

"I cry when I am angry," she whispered to herself. "I don't want Jack to cry." The thought of him blubbering at his desk somehow made her feel afraid. If someone like Jack the Giant Killer could be broken, how could she ever hope to stay strong?

The bell rang, and it was time for recess. It was too cold to go outside, so the class lined up and made their way to the gym with its tall metal rafters and bouncy gray floor. A teacher there had balls and mats ready to play a game. The mats, which the teacher called bases, were laid out in a square. The students would kick the ball and then run and touch the bases. It sounded way too easy, so Jaika knew there must be more to the rules.

Again, she tried to listen, but found herself staring at Jack instead. He had found a seat to himself in the back corner of the gym. A few older students sat on the ground along the back wall doing book work. They looked just as unhappy as Jack. Rosie pointed to them and explained that students in trouble do not get to play games. They must sit and work, which completely explained their unhappiness. Nick shook his head in disapproval. Jaika was sure he had a scientific reason for their behavior that he was keeping to himself.

Jaika

The game was progressing and soon Jaika took her turn. The pitcher rolled the ball, and she kicked it with all her strength. A boy in a blue shirt caught it and threw it at Jaika, striking her square in the back.

"You're out!" shouted another student.

Jaika shook off her embarrassment and tried to ignore the stinging sensation between her shoulders. The missing rules were now becoming quite clear. She would not make that mistake again.

She ran to take her seat beside her friends, but Rosie and Nick weren't watching the game. They were watching Jack. The older boys were no longer seated by the back wall. Instead, they stood towering over Jack in the far corner, his eyes wide with fear as he wiped the sweat from his face. The tallest boy shook his fist at Jack. His face turned red as he shouted unintelligible words at the cowering Giant Killer. He stepped closer to Jack and then raised his fist to strike. Jack put his hands up over his face to block the impending blow. It was all too much. Jaika thought of her nights spent hiding in the lower rooms of her father's castle, listening to Inita tell stories or sing songs to cover the sounds in the upper rooms. The sounds of soldiers leaving and returning from battle. She thought of her first night in this world. She thought of the raging water that had almost killed her and of the sad people in her father's castle after an attack. No one should have to be afraid. No matter who they are – even someone like Jack.

Jaika could hear her heart pounding in her ears. Her hands closed into fists, and before she could think anymore, she ran. She ran toward this new giant and threw her full weight against his legs. He heard the crack of her shoulder bone striking his knee. Her tiny body crumpled to the floor, but the giant did not move. He only looked annoyed.

Rosie gasped. "No! Jaika, stop!" She ran to Jaika's side and threw her arms around her friend, protecting her from the giant. "Her father is a king!"

Everyone else ran too. In fact, everyone in the gym ran straight to the far corner.

Voices chanted, "Fight! Fight! Fight!"

Jaika and Rosie glared up at this new giant. Fear, anger, and gravity cemented them to each other as well as the gym floor. They were not moving. The giant knew he could squash them with one blow. He growled at the girls and shook his fist – but he did not strike. Jaika watched his eyes cloud over with confusion. No doubt he could not understand why these insignificant girls would protect Jack. Jack, who tortured and berated other students, the same Jack who mocked, and kicked, and spat on smaller people. Why was he worth protecting?

Jaika didn't really understand why she had done it, so of course this new giant couldn't understand either. She just knew it was the right thing to do. Everyone should be safe – even Jack.

"If he's a king, why are you here in this dirt hole of a school?"

Jaika stared back at the giant not sure how to answer.

Rosie stood up and helped Jaika to her feet. Nick was in the crowd shaking his head, just as confused as everyone else. The teacher intervened and drove everyone out of the corner and back to the game. The new giant and Jack were sent to the office to face dire consequences.

Jaika didn't want to play anymore. She just wanted to go home. She wanted to see her father and Ree and the Manchura trees. She wanted Inita back and Gali, so she would feel safe again. She walked out of the gym, down the hall, and straight to the front door of the school. The tall windows allowed her to see all the way down the sidewalk into the street. There was a red wooden bench by the office door, and Jaika would wait there. Mattie would come, or her father would come. Someone would come to take her away from the giants.

Someone did come. A delicate lady in a pale green dress. "You must be Jaika."

Jaika nodded.

"I am Mrs. Stafford. I have been told that you are very brave."

Jaika burst into tears. She certainly didn't feel brave. Mrs. Stafford sat down beside her on the red bench and thought about what to say.

"Can you tell me what happened?"

"No one believes me," Jaika sobbed.

Mrs. Stafford bit her lip to fight back a laugh. She had expected this tiny girl to talk about almost being hit or in a fight. To discuss a boy three times her size towering over her in anger, or the whole gym watching her.

"Believe what?" Mrs. Stafford's voice was warm and gentle.

Jaika turned to get a better look at this new ally.

"They don't believe that my father is a king."

"I see," Mrs. Stafford hid her surprise. "And is it important that they believe you?"

Jaika shrugged. She'd never really thought about it before. "Shouldn't it be important?"

"Even if no one believes you, won't he still be a king?" Mrs. Stafford raised her eyebrow in a very knowledgeable way.

Jaika thought about her words. Whatever people thought about her father wouldn't make any difference. He would still be king. Even if Mrs. Stafford didn't believe.

"Yes," Jaika agreed, "yes he will." Her face beamed with her announcement. "He will be king no matter what they say."

"Would it really matter if he wasn't a king? Would it change who you are? Would it make you sad?"

Jaika stared at this kind lady in the green dress. She couldn't possibly understand how important her father was. But her words were filled with truth. She would still be Jaika. No matter what her father did or where he lived, she would not be any different.

"I guess not," she said taking a deep breath. "And... what if there weren't any blue people with wings or golden people with white hair?"

The counselor studied Jaika, impressed with her imagination. "Yes, Jaika, if there were no blue people or gold people, would that change you? Would that make you any different?"

Jaika closed her eyes for a moment. "There aren't any blue people here, are there?"

"Well I have never seen any. I don't suppose there aren't any, just none that I have seen. So maybe, just for now, only you and I should talk about your father and the blue people. You can tell me about his castle and your home, but it can be our secret. Would that be okay?"

Jaika understood. To tell people that her father was a king — to tell people that she had walked through a watery wall of light would only make things worse. So Ree, and Inita, and Gali, and her father would have to live in her heart. She would keep them close to her as her secret because she was here now. She was in a new place, and she would make a new life. She tried to be brave, the way Ree would want her to, but she would never give up hope that she might see them again.

"Our secret," she whispered.

Jaika knew she must not talk about this secret anymore. Rosie and Nick knew, and Mattie knew, and now this kind lady, but she would have to try and not remember so much. It seemed to make people angry or sad. For now, she would let go of her home, and her father, and Ree. For now, she would only think about her new friends. But just for now...

Jaika promised to come see Mrs. Stafford every day for a while, at least until she was feeling better.

Birthday

Mattie finished the last smear of icing on the third layer of their molten lava chocolate cake. In years past, she had decorated their birthday cake with fluorescent colored sprinkles or ribbons of red or pink icing around the top edges. One year they even stuck real flowers on the top. This year, however, they had agreed. This year would be a sophisticated birthday – a simple afternoon shared with friends. Mattie would be turning 84 and Jaika would be 17, or at least that's what they estimated. Without written records, no one knew the exact date of Jaika's birthday much less her age, so she had chosen to celebrate with Mattie. On her school records, her official birthday was January 18th — the same date as Mattie's.

Jaika looked down at her blue pendant. She knew Mattie was not her real mother, but she had no memory of another, except the pale woman who had worn the pendant. Time had taken much of Regar from her memories. On occasion, she still ran through the Regarian flower trees with a brave, young boy — but only in her dreams. The watery nightmares had long since passed, and only shadows of faces remained.

Once the icing was smooth, Mattie handed the spatula to Jaika. "Eighty-four years is a long time to be alive," Jaika mused, licking the chocolate from the corner of her mouth.

"It went by so fast," Mattie nodded and sat down in one of the kitchen chairs. "So very fast..." She closed her eyes and took a deep breath. "Where did it all go?"

Jaika had watched her friend slowing down a little more every day, but she would never have said that out loud — longer naps, repeated stories, fewer days spent in the garden. She knew ignoring the truth wouldn't change it, but somehow it made it a little easier to face. Jaika did most of the cooking and housework now. Mattie did not ask for help, but little by little, Jaika had taken up one chore and then another, preparing evening meals while Mattie napped in her favorite rocking chair. Just making the cake had left her exhausted. There would not be many more birthdays to celebrate. Mattie was aging and next year Jaika would go away to college. Everything was changing.

Rosie and Jack arrived at two o'clock precisely. Rosie in her camouflage pants and Jack in his red number 12 Jersey. Nick, however, was late. He was always late. There was always one more thing to do, one more person to save, one more experiment to complete. Nevertheless, if Jaika had to pick a friend to take to the ends of the Earth, it probably would have been Nick. Jack was fearless and strong and Rosie would never let her down, but Nick was so level headed. He knew just what to do when everyone was upset or angry. He had become the rock they could all lean against. She wished she could be more like Nick. She hoped the others hadn't noticed how close they had become, or the secret smiles of understanding they shared when no one was looking. The way he would brush his fingertips along her arm or cheek when they talked. Yes, Nick was her favorite.

He would be leaving soon as well. A big college up north had accepted his application for engineering school. She had already forgotten the name. Nick's mile-wide grin when he was accepted, however, would stay with her forever.

Jack stuck his finger in the icing, watching Mattie for a reprimand. Mattie looked around the room but did not respond. Jaika wondered just how much she could really see. The cataracts were thick now. There would be shapes and light, but she could never be sure how much detail was really clear. Mattie was too stubborn to let the doctors help her. Those doctors don't know what they are doing, she would say.

Nick finally arrived in his quiet, reassuring manner – tucked in shirt and linen jacket. Rosie took his arrival as the signal to cut the cake. No one bothered to sing or light a candle. This was the last birthday party they would share, and everyone could feel the end coming. Rosie talked about her dad. He was looking at a house in another city. He thought a change of scenery would be good for both of them. The Marines was the next step for her, so it didn't really matter where they lived.

Jack was playing football. He was three times the size of any one in this room and had truly become a giant. He was playing defense for their high school, and he would play in college under a full scholarship. Jaika was incredibly proud of Jack. He never told her all the reasons for the way he had acted in the past — the anger — the cruelty — but she was proud of him anyway. His past didn't matter. Maybe they would talk about it someday.

Jaika served herself an extra-large slice of cake and a smaller piece for Mattie. "Would you like some help?" Jaika put a fork in Mattie's hand.

Mattie nodded, looking past the people in the room. "Steven, Steven where have you been? Why were you so late?"

Rosie patted Mattie on the shoulder. "There is no Steven here, Mattie. There's Nick and there's Jack, but no Steven."

"Your uniform is so dirty," said Mattie. "Where have you been?"

Jaika turned and looked in the direction that Mattie

was staring. "There's no one there, Mattie. Who are you talking to?"

Mattie smiled, but did not answer.

Nick touched Jaika's arm. "I think there is something wrong."

"She's fine," Jaika argued. "She is just seeing shadows."

"Mattie," Nick questioned softly, "who are you talking to?"

She reached a shaky hand toward the back wall of the kitchen. "My Steven," she breathed.

Jaika froze. There was no Steven there. There was no one there at all. The only Steven Mattie had ever talked about was in a faded photograph. An old photograph she kept in the drawer of her night stand. A photograph of a man in uniform who was...

"Mattie?" Jaika called. "Are you okay?"

She did not answer.

Nick took hold of Jaika's arm. "Call 911," he urged. "We need to call 911 now."

Jaika did not like the idea, but she wasn't sure what else to do. Mattie was not herself. "She's fine," Jaika argued, "just confused." She didn't like the possibility that something was wrong, something unfixable, something unstoppable.

Nick called 911 anyway.

Jaika went to Mattie. She dropped to her knees, and put her hands in Mattie's lap. "Mattie, there is no Steven here."

"My Jaika," she whispered, looking without seeing. "Thank you for loving me."

She wasn't smiling any more. Her breath was short and shallow, choppy like someone who had been running. Jaika stroked her leg and told her not to worry. "It's going to be okay, Mattie. It's going to be okay."

Mattie's eyes closed and she began to slump sideways in the chair. Jaika put her hands against her frail body to support her and yelled for help. Jack was there in a heartbeat, lifting Mattie up like a tattered rag doll. He carried her to the back of the house and laid her on the bed.

She was so still. Jaika couldn't see her chest moving anymore.

Jaika went to the small table beside the bed and opened the drawer. Mattie still kept the picture there. The picture of her son and her husband. Maybe he was the man she had seen, Jaika thought, in the kitchen, in the dirty uniform. She laid the picture beside her and held onto her Mattie's hand.

There was a coolness to her skin now. The place where Jaika held her arm was cool. There was still a hint of warmth to her body, but life was leaving, she could feel it. It was going out of her — out of the ceiling — out of the roof of the house. Maybe Steven was with her. She hoped Steven was with her. Mattie shouldn't be alone. She need someone to take care of her.

Nick let the paramedics in the front door. They came into the bedroom and immediately set to work. Jaika watched the man in white lift Mattie's eyelid and shine a light into her glassy, lifeless eyes. Those eyes that saw nothing. Mattie was gone and Jaika didn't want to be here either.

Nick spoke with the man in the white shirt, explaining what he had seen. Rosie sat in the kitchen with Jack but couldn't think of any way to help.

Jaika was out the front door before anyone could stop her. The sun was so bright. It's warmth on her skin felt wrong and out of place. How could the world still look so normal? The flowers, the trees, the birds, the people on the street. Didn't they know the world was ending?

Jaika kept going down the long sidewalk. The sidewalk that surrounded every block of houses, broken only by the intersection of the crossing streets.

She wasn't walking anymore. She was running. She couldn't think. She couldn't feel, but she could run. At the end of the block, she turned. If she kept going, the highway would be just ahead, endless cars, noise, people, somewhere other than here.

Her legs ached but she couldn't stop, as if running could help Mattie in some way. When the toe of her shoe hooked the crack in the sidewalk, Jaika didn't care. She didn't even try to stop her fall. She landed in the grass of some stranger's lawn... and sobbed. The waves of tears were unstoppable. Just like Mattie's death, there was nothing in this world that could make it better. And nothing else beyond that mattered... not the mud that caked her clothes from the wet lawn, not the blood that oozed from her knees, not college, not Jack or Rosie or Nick... nothing.

When the giant lifted her from the ground, she didn't fight. He lifted her higher than even Jack could have managed. His arms like boulders. He held her like a child against his chest. She could smell sweat and dirt. His chest was slick and covered only with leather straps that crisscrossed his oily skin. Jaika thought he looked like a bandito from an old movie wearing ammunition belts. Maybe he would kill her, or maybe even worse. It didn't matter. Nothing mattered.

She lost consciousness as he carried her through the wall of light. She didn't see Jack or Nick running toward them, only her Azura pendant glowing with blue fire.

Prison

A misty gray light filtered through the window in the wooden door of Jaika's cell. Not a window, exactly, more like a hole cut in the top part of the door. Just a slender rectangle of a hole in a giant door. It would take three men to move that door, she thought, staring at the sliver of light on the stone floor. The light from the window was the only light in the empty room — at least she hoped it was empty.

From flat on her back, Jaika listened and strained to see into the dark corners of the room. Her hands were shackled together across her stomach. The metal cut into her wrists and made her fingers turn blue. Rolling over onto her shoulder, Jaika pushed herself to a sitting position still studying the inky dark corners around her.

Her muscles groaned from the time spent unconscious on the icy, stone floor. Her bare feet numb and lifeless, much like the rocks on the walls and floor.

99

Her clothes were still wet and muddy. The room was cold and the air stale, her body stiff and her stomach empty, but worst of all Jaika had no idea where she was.

She remembered a wall of light and a giant man...and Mattie. The coldness in the room came rushing into her chest and back and the hollowness of yesterday returned. Jaika could not stop the memory of Mattie's cold staring eyes. The EMT shining his pen light as if he could find her soul way down inside those eyes. She thought about Rosie and Nick and Jack, and suddenly she didn't care where she was anymore. It didn't matter who was here or where here was. Mattie wasn't ever coming home so Jaika had no reason to go home either.

Keys rattled in the hallway. Jaika scooted back into the shadows as the massive door creaked open. A man appeared in the doorway blocking out most of the outside light. She could barely see his face in the dimness, but she was sure this man in the doorway was the same man who had carried her through the light and to this horrible place.

"Notch dir," nodded her captor in a business-as-usual tone. "Garik tow barok." He looked into the darkness. Jaika didn't think he could see her, but she had the odd feeling he knew she was there just the same.

His words were strange, certainly not from any language Jaika had ever heard. His broad shoulders almost touched the sides of the doorway as he entered the cell. His chest was bare, and he wore the same black pants and shoulder strapped uniform as the day before. Careful not to turn his back to Jaika, he laid a metal plate and cup in the middle of the floor and left without speaking another word, dragging the door closed behind him.

Jaika crawled out of the darkness across the stone floor to examine her gift. The cup was filled with water, and the plate held bread and some sort of yellow fruit. Maybe it would be poisoned she thought, and then she wouldn't have to face this place or Mattie's death.

Jaika shivered in the darkness, thinking of her empty house and the uneaten birthday cake. Her bonds made it difficult to turn her hands. She grasped the food with her right hand then turned her head to eat with the side of her mouth, fruit juice dripping down her chin. The fruit was sweet but there wasn't enough water. She titled the cup and let the last few drops trickle out.

Her jailer must have been watching through the window because as soon as she finished the last of the bread the door opened. He pulled Jaika to her feet and motioned for her to follow him out into the hallway. Jaika staggered behind the soldier trying to shake the stiffness from her legs. They passed rows of identical doors as they walked. Wooden doors she thought might have been other jail cells. They each had the same slit of a window as the door to her cell. Jaika listened for voices behind the doors, but the only sounds were their echoing footsteps.

Fiery torches hung in wrought iron racks outside each door. Oily, foul-smelling torches that gave off little light, and certainly no warmth. The hallway walls were all carved out of the same gray stone as her cell, and there were no windows to the outside world at all. This could have been a dungeon out of any story filled with knights and castles and damsels in distress.

The end of the hallway held a stairway and still another wooden door. This door led into a large room with very simple furnishings. The walls held a single shield and the floor was covered with a rough, woolly brown rug. A faded tapestry hung on the back wall depicting a battle won. Dead bodies scattered the edges of the scene. Candles burned in black sconces along one wall.

A second door at the back of the room opened to admit a tall, willowy lady with pale blue skin that glowed against the ugly stone walls. She walked toward Jaika with an angelic sway almost as if she were walking on air. Her rail thin arms floated open in welcome. Her right hand carried a long white cloth.

Jaika could not help but stare into her eyes, round, blue eyes, ocean blue, deeper blue than her skin, but painted with the same hues. Her hair was long and blue-white. Its silky strands floated like water along her shoulders and back. She wore a satiny white sheath that moved as gently as she did. The dress could easily have been part of her body. And attached to her shoulders and back, or maybe part of the dress, was a set of wings.

At least Jaika thought they looked like wings. Blue, paper thin wings crisscrossed with tiny veins and held together with a pencil thin framework. They hugged her body, disappearing against her like a sleeping sparrow, but they fluttered slightly now and again as she moved.

Jaika glanced over her shoulder at her jailer. "Just wanted to make sure you were still there, and that this was all real... this blue lady person."

The giant did not laugh. His eyes were cold and lifeless like that of a mannequin in a department store window.

The woman nodded at her two visitors and removed a key from her pocket. With nimble fingers, she removed Jaika's wristbands then handed her the cloth and pointed to a wooden screen at the far side of the room. "Please go behind there and change my dear."

Jaika's heart started to race. Until this moment she had not cared what happened to her. With Mattie gone, the future was so dark. Nothing was important anymore. But this blue woman changed everything. There were no blue people on Earth... were there?

"You speak English?" Jaika charged. "Where am I?"

"Yes, my dear. Now please go and change. Your clothes are dirty."

"But where am I...?"

The elegant lady smiled and looked at Torin. They

shared a look of painful understanding, the weight of a memory no one dared speak about. She nodded to the man, and Torin left, making sure the door shut behind him.

There was no place to run, and this woman seemed harmless enough, so Jaika complied. Behind the screen, Jaika discovered the cloth was, in fact, a dress. A slim, linen tunic which fit loosely over her head. After trading her muddy clothes for the tunic, she emerged from the screen. The woman tied a thin rope around her waist and nodded her approval.

"Torin will be back for you later."

"Torin," said Jaika staring up into those bottomless eyes. "Is that his name?"

"Yes. And I am Seela," announced the woman. "I will be your teacher." She turned to stare at the door where Torin had left, providing Jaika with a clear view of her delicate wings. "I will teach you to speak the language of our city."

"Are there many languages on this... I mean... here?" Jaika desperately wanted to know where she was and was excited to hear words she could understand. Maybe this lady could help her.

"Regar. The name of our world is Regar." Seela finally turned to study Jaika. She was fighting to maintain a clinical demeanor.

Jaika felt a little like a rat in a lab. "Regar," she said.

"What's a Regar?"

Seela tried not to smile. The other girls had been just as shocked, but there was no need to tell her about the others. She would find out soon enough. "It is a world, my dear, different than Earth, but still the same."

Jaika wished Rosie and Nick could see this blue lady. "The blue fairy," mumbled Jaika while truly wishing Pinocchio and Jiminy Cricket would appear. At least they would be people she recognized. "Are there many blue people here... on Regar?"

"Once," Seela sighed. "Once we were many. The Tal were a peaceful, gentle..."

Jaika watched the weighted memories crush this elegant lady and take her thoughts far from this room, and for a moment, Seela looked completely lost.

"You need to learn to speak Regarian," Seela returned to the business at hand. "It is the dominant language on this world. When Kaleus returns, he will have questions for you."

"Kaleus?"

"Our... king."

Seela stumbled on the word 'king.' Jaika wondered if it was a translation flaw or something else altogether.

"Now let us begin."

Kaleus

For the next two weeks, Jaika spent her waking hours with Seela. Each day's routine was much like the day's before. In the morning, Torin brought a simple breakfast and a clean, full-length tunic but never any shoes. Jaika was allowed to bathe and change in a tiny closet-sized room across the hallway. The stone floor was always cold on her bare feet. But even in there, bathing and changing, she was never left unguarded. Torin was always a breath away.

Jaika never really felt afraid or threatened, but a continual promise of doom hung over her constant routines. She couldn't help but feel a little like a turkey being fattened up for Thanksgiving, but just what holiday lay ahead was unknown.

Torin might as well have been a robot. His jingling keys always warned of his approach, but when he arrived he said very little. Those few words, as Jaika learned, were words Mattie would have never let her repeat. He never struck her, but there was no doubt in her mind that he would not hesitate to kill her when the time came. It would only take one blow.

The Regarian language came quickly for Jaika. The words were familiar like an old pair of jeans. Words she knew but had not used in such a long time.

Seela was patient. She praised Jaika for her work and tried to make her as comfortable as possible. Seela would often bring a sweet treat or special drink to make her lesson more tolerable. Asking too many questions, however, was not tolerated. So Jaika would listen quietly and wonder what it would be like to fly.

Dressing, eating, language study, they never ventured any further than the dismal hallway. This routine continued for fifteen days. Jaika scratched a mark on the door each evening to keep count. But, on the fifteenth day, everything changed.

Torin was in an even worse temper than usual that morning. He spilled most of her breakfast and yelled at Jaika to hurry. At least that's what she thought he said. Even Seela seemed nervous and tense. Something was definitely going on.

"You will be taken to meet Kaleus today," smiled Seela at the beginning of their morning lesson. "It is a great honor to serve him."

"Kaleus?" Jaika settled back in a rickety, wooden

chair. She was tired of never getting any answers.

"He is the ruler of this realm. He is a very powerful king." Her words came in short, quick bursts, and she paced as she spoke making her wings flex and flutter, "I hope he will be pleased with you."

"Pleased?" Jaika gave Seela a bewildered look.

"Yes, the others did not please him." Seela's eyes clouded as she spoke.

"Others? What others?" Jaika slid to the edge of her chair starting to worry.

"The others that I have taught our language." She could not even look at Jaika anymore. "None have learned as quickly as you. He will be pleased. I know he will." She tried to sound convincing.

"And if he's not?"

Seela's body tensed. Slowly she sat down in the chair beside Jaika. It didn't matter anymore. Today Jaika's life would change, so there was no more need for secrets.

"Two other girls have been brought to me for training. Two other girls who spoke your language," Seela closed her eyes at their memory. "The words are my gift," she continued.

"I don't understand."

"Language is my gift. I can see the words you speak, and I know what you say."

"So everyone that looks like you has this gift?"

Seela chuckled. "Looks like me?"

"You know, the whole blue with wings thing."

"My people are Tal. Many of my people have gifts. In my family are healers and those who see the rhythms, the patterns in the world, in the languages, in the pictures, in the people. We see the patterns."

"So there are people in your family that can fix people when they are hurt?"

"Yes... my daughter, Ilea, was a healer. She was a strong healer. She could change you with only a touch."

"I would like to meet her," Jaika decided, thinking about Mattie and how she could have been saved.

"I am afraid that will not be possible." Seela stood and fought the emptiness in her heart. "Oberon sent her away with the SolStone."

"He killed her?" Jaika sat straight in her chair, already hating this guy Oberon. She wasn't sure who he was, but for now she wanted to learn more about Seela.

"No, if she were dead, at least I would know where she was." Seela paced the tiny training room deciding just how much to tell Jaika. "He brought you here with the SolStone, the SolStone that sent Ilea away."

Jaika sighed. There was so much she didn't understand. "What's a SolStone?"

"When you were brought to Regar, you came through the light."

"Yes," Jaika almost jumped. Finally, she was finding answers. "Yes, Torin carried me through."

"That was by the power of the SolStone. Oberon controls the SolStone."

"I still don't understand." Jaika covered her eyes with her hands and puffed her breath.

"It's a blue gem stone that can be used to open a doorway to other worlds. It was broken many turns ago, but Oberon has found most of the pieces. That is how you were brought here, and I believe it is how you left. If you are truly the one he seeks."

Jaika thought about the wall of light and Torin ...and her pendant. She could see it's glow in her memory from the night Torin captured her. Maybe he had taken it. Maybe it was a SolStone. Maybe it could take her home. "So what happened to your daughter?"

"Oberon did not understand the SolStone. He needed to test it, to find out how it worked. He used our children." Seela took a ragged breath and Jaika could see her hands begin to shake. "He used the children of our planet to test his SolStone. The children of Regar – so many children — sent wherever the SolStone chose."

"So Oberon sent your daughter somewhere?"

"Yes, he used her to test his stone. I do not know if she lives, and if she lives, I do not know where. My hope is that she is safe."

"Maybe Earth, like me." Jaika whispered,

remembering.

"Do you have a husband?" Jaika asked, not wanting Seela to quit talking.

"No, only my son. He works in the crystal mines. That is why I do this." Seela looked away, ashamed of her cruelty and cowardice. "If we can make Kaleus happy. If we can bring him... you... if you are truly the girl he seeks, we can have our children back. It is all he desires in this world, to find you, to fulfill the prophecy."

"What prophecy?"

Jaika could feel Seela getting nervous. "We should return to the lesson. You must be able to answer his questions if he speaks to you."

"If he speaks to me?"

"Yes. He uses Oberon to do most of his work. It is seldom that Kaleus speaks directly to anyone. Kaleus or Oberon, it will not matter. When they speak, you must answer."

"And if I answer incorrectly?"

Seela did not have to explain. Jaika understood exactly what would happen. She completely understood what had happened to the other girls Seela had trained. Her muscles shivered at the thought.

The morning's lesson wore on forever. Jaika couldn't keep her mind focused. She kept thinking about Kaleus. *Why is everyone afraid of him? And what does he want with me?* She kept thinking of the story books Mattie had read to her. Cinderella, Camelot, all of those kings were handsome and kind. Kaleus was definitely not a story book king.

After lunch, Seela brought a change of clothes. She brushed Jaika's hair away from her face and secured it with a brassy clip, rebellious curls escaping around her face. Then, she helped her dress in a silvery gown. The sleeves were long and the neck was open to the shoulder. A long belt fitted the waist, swinging against her legs as she walked...as she walked that afternoon with Torin, cold bare feet, down the long, gray hall toward Kaleus. Jaika was sure her heart would burst with every footstep.

Together, they climbed the stairway outside Seela's classroom. At the top was another world. It was nothing like the cold, stone rooms that Jaika had spent the last two weeks in. Here the walls were smooth, sparkling, and warm. Large windows lined the walls revealing a breathtaking view of the gardens, and allowing generous amounts of sunlight to soak into every corner of the hallway. The outside world was filled with rainbow-colored flowers and glowing trees of green and yellow. The air smelled fresh and clean. Jaika even noticed a door or two that led out into this wonderland.

Somewhere along the way, she turned to watch Torin following close behind. His presence seemed to dim the beauty outside the windows.

Glowing plants grew tall in yellow and red window

boxes along the base of the walls. Damaged swords and weapons covered the shimmering hallway. Small butterfly like creatures flitted about her head making odd musical sounds. Most were gold in color, but a few were pink or purple. Jaika swatted one that whistled in her ear. *It's bad luck to kill a wingaring,* she thought. *Now why do I know that?*

Until they reached the guards outside the throne room, there were no other people. Two, stone-faced, uniformed guards opened the massive doors that led to Kaleus's throne. Twelve foot, double doors opened into a cavernous meeting hall. A domed ceiling painted with clouds and sky floated high above them. Enormous, white columns stood in rank along the sides of the room. People lined the walls behind the columns twittering and laughing at some undisclosed joke reminding Jaika of an orchestra's chaotic tuning before a performance.

Jaika was taken to the middle of the room and seated on a wooden bench. She thought about the other girls Seela had trained. Had they sat on this very bench before... him.

Torin stood behind her. His heart beat as wildly as her own. She could feel the throbbing of his pulse in the leg he shoved against her back.

The bench faced an elevated platform which filled the back wall and held a mammoth, silver throne. It was covered with shining stones and cast a powerful shadow. There were only four steps leading up to the platform, but even these sparkled and gleamed. Two narrow, black banners hung behind the throne. Jaika could not make out the odd writing, but the pictures were of crossed swords.

A trumpet sounded, and a distant tower bell tolled.

Jaika held her breath.

A thin, cloaked figure emerged from behind the throne. His movements were so subtle he appeared to float across the platform. The restless crowd began to chant. "Kaleus! Kaleus!"

The stranger removed his hood to reveal sleek, black hair and a shortly clipped beard and mustache. Raising a gloved hand to the crowd, the room fell silent. No one dared to disobey. With a patient nod, he quietly crossed in front of the throne to wait on the opposite side.

Jaika let out a gasp. She had not taken a breath since the strange man took the stage. She watched him, standing beside the throne, staring straight at her. This must be the man who had taken Seela's daughter.

The crowd looked beyond him, past the throne, toward the shadows behind. Anticipation and fear rose toward the cloud-painted ceiling. White smoke boiled from the platform steps, and the crowd began to cheer again. Red sparks fired from the smoke, and a shadowy figure appeared behind it.

Nauseating fear swept over Jaika.

As the smoke cleared, a man dressed in velvety robes, took his place on the throne. He moved slowly, almost dreamlike, and it was difficult to tell his age. His tight-fitting pants and tunic revealed powerful muscles. His boots came up to his knee, and the toes were covered in silver. His hair was red-brown, slicked back and tied. Once seated, he stared out at the crowd with unfeeling eyes.

"Quite a show," whispered Jaika trying hard to be brave.

The man on the throne motioned, and the bearded man beside him dropped his cape to the floor and moved forward. He was dressed entirely in black and wore a jagged, almost circular pendant that shone with a pale blue light.

"Bring the daughter of the prophesy!" He commanded. His words rumbled over the cheering crowd.

Jaika was pushed from her seat and told to greet the king. Torin shoved his knee into Jaika's back, pushing her forward to stand in front of the platform. Surprisingly, Kaleus did not move. He stared out at the crowd in apathy. Oberon, however, moved forward, devouring Jaika with his eyes. Slowly, methodically, he scanned every detail of her face and body. Jaika shivered as though she could feel his eyes touching her skin.

With a frustrated shake of his head, the king picked up a weapon from the arm of the throne and fired it into the crowd. Sparks flew, and a man on the edge of the crowd vanished. For an instant, the room was silent, everyone held their breath until Oberon turned his attention back toward Jaika.

Jaika stepped back only to bump into Torin and the bench. Her heart pounded as Oberon moved closer. Jaika turned to run, but Torin caught her arm. As he pulled her back, she saw the unmistakable fear in his eyes. If the giant Torin was afraid of this man, then there was no hope.

Her breath came in short gasps. Oberon grabbed her arm, and spun her back against him. He jerked her forward and pushed her hair to the side. With a loud rip, he yanked the sleeve of her dress to completely expose her left shoulder. The crowd cheered even louder than before.

"No!" She shouted, struggling to free herself. Oberon buried his fingers deep into her arm. Jaika winced with the pain. She could feel his hot breath as he studied the birth mark along her shoulder blade.

Without loosening his grip, Oberon softly lowered his lips to her neck in a burning kiss. "My Picari," he whispered against her skin. "I have found you."

Fear split her body as he turned her face to his. His square jaw was marked by an ugly red scar across his left cheek, and his eyes seems to drill straight through her...blue eyes...cold, unfeeling, ice blue eyes.

116

For a moment, Jaika thought he would kill her.

Then Oberon broke into an evil smile and began to laugh. "I have found her!" he roared. "Begin the training!" he commanded and flung Jaika into Torin's arms.

The bell began to ring again, and the crowd roared their approval. The sound was deafening as Torin pulled her back to the entrance. She clung weakly to his arm whimpering until they cleared the double doors.

Then she ran.

With all her strength, she flew down the empty hallway. Reaching the first door, she was out.

Her actions caught Torin by complete surprise, and he stared in disbelief, but only for a moment. Years of training took over, and he pursued like a well-oiled machine.

Only several feet from the door, Jaika entered the gardens. She cut a path through the dense trees, stumbling in the vines. The bushes tore at her dress and cut into her legs and bare feet.

Then, like a stone wall, the garden ended. Jaika collapsed to her knees as she stared out at the desert wasteland that lay before her. Nothing but sand and sun for miles. Except for the brilliance of the sun, she could have been staring at any of Earth's deserts. There was nowhere to go — no escape.

"Bartok!" Torin growled as he entwined his

fingers in her hair and lifted Jaika to her feet. "If I lose you, my wife will be executed," he sputtered in broken Regarian. "I will kill you before I let you escape. Is that clear?" He drew back his fist to strike, but hesitated, taking a deep, angry breath.

Torin did not wait for her to answer. Half-dragging and half-walking, they returned together through the garden and into the shining castle. Down the stairs he pulled her. Away from the warm windows and delicate flowers. Away from the sunlit walls and cheering crowds. Back to the dark chambers below and to her cold prison.

Torin slapped metal shackles on her wrists and shoved her into the cell. The heavy door slammed and the lock slid into place, booming against the empty walls. Then, the room fell silent. She could hear the jingle of keys as Torin walked away.

Jaika collapsed to the floor in tears, shivering in defeat. There was nowhere to go, no escape. Nothing beyond the walls and the garden. No one knew where she was. Even she didn't know. She had nothing but a dark cell and the rattle of Torin's keys.

Training

"Wait up!" shouted Richard, crossing the courtyard in long easy strides. He wore the disheveled appearance of a man just out of bed. Shaggy, uncombed hair, crumpled black pants and a fighting tunic that looked fresh off of the bedroom floor, but his youthful, good-natured grin softened all the wrinkles.

Richard had just left his soldier's quarters and was heading toward Kaleus's castle. Its towers shone white against the magnificent yellows and reds of the gardens that surrounded the walls. Mossy blue plants covered the courtyard's grounds and snaked in-between most of the smaller buildings — basic rock and wood structures for the less important staff. He couldn't help but smile at the extravagance around him. Kaleus certainly knew how to live well.

"We're going to be late," scolded Davin with his usual scowl. "Don't you know what today is?" He never let his companion forget who was in charge.

He wore the same uniform as his partner, but they could not have been more different. Like day and night, Davin's crisp appearance balanced Richard's chaos. His short-cropped hair and flawless attire made his partner look even more rumbled when they stood side by side. Davin knew Richard was an usually skilled fighter, but his childish antics and messy appearance annoyed him to no end.

"Of course I remember." Richard's blue eyes sparkled as he stomped childishly on a yellow Mantika flower. "I have been looking forward to this – the official princess has arrived," he announced to no one. "I hear she's even escaped once or twice. She'll make a great fighter."

"Swordsman," corrected Davin impatiently, running his hand along his chin. "She'll be lucky if she can lift the thing."

"Swordsman," whispered Richard in a falsely deep voice, amused at his teacher's grave expression. He reveled in annoying Davin.

Once they were inside, Richard quickly remembered how fond he was of Kaleus's castle. The inside was even more glorious than the outer gardens. There was no shortage of crystals in Kaleus's court. The stone walls glowed with warmth absorbed from crystal powered lighting. Heaters blazed in the colder rooms of the upper levels. Crystal shards were ground into plant food to keep not only the gardens lush but the pottery grown vines and ferns that lined the hallways and galleries and crept up Kaleus's shining walls.

They made their way through the high-ceilinged entryway toward the training rooms. Rooms with weapons and shields. Rooms where peasants could be made into soldiers. Rooms where Davin and Richard would meet their new apprentice.

Richard kept asking questions, but Davin wasn't listening anymore.

#

Torin shook the sleep from Jaika's tired bones and placed her breakfast on the floor. From the slam of the door, she knew he was still angry at her attempted escape. There would be no forgiveness from this man.

She ate in silence in her cell until Seela appeared with a short, white tunic and a pair of tight fitting pants. She even provided a pair of black boots. Jaika's toes felt trapped after the endless days of bare feet.

After Jaika was dressed, Torin placed a flexible, copper-colored band around her neck.

"This will stop any more escapes," Torin assured her.

She could tell by the look on his face that it was

true, everything he said was true. She followed him down the hallway to the stairs. The same stairs she had climbed to meet Kaleus and Oberon the day before.

As they neared the first floor, Torin thrust a small silver box in her face. "This controls you now. Your collar has rare fire crystals. They will... they will burn..." he stammered. "The box makes a sound... then they burn." Torin swallowed hard.

Jaika raised her hand to touch the metal around her neck. "Burn," she whispered and nodded her understanding.

Torin led the way down the shimmering hallway of the upper level. A rock, hard lump settled deep in Jaika's stomach. There would be no escape today, maybe never.

They passed the double doors of the great hall and continued on to a smaller section of the castle. Here the ceilings were not as high, and the decor was sparse. They passed several staircases, so Jaika knew there were more floors and more rooms in this terrible place, but she could only guess at how many.

"What's her name?" Jaika asked in a tentative voice trying desperately to appease her captor.

Torin did not answer, nor did he slow his pace.

"Your wife." Jaika repeated. "What's your wife's name?"

Torin stopped in front of one of the many doors along the hallway. It was different only in the circular emblem burned into the center — two swords crossed with a broken star beneath.

"Mara." He spoke her name with no emotion, his eyes empty and cold. He opened the door and shoved Jaika through.

The training room resembled a large gymnasium. The ceiling was three men high, and the floor was flexible. Jaika was sure she could bounce on it if she tried. It was rectangular in shape and the two longer walls were solid reflective metal, like mirrors. A shoulder high box made from that same reflective metal protruded from the floor at the back of the room.

"Welcome, my lady," stated Davin with a sweeping bow. His build and dark hair bore a striking resemblance to the king, or was it Oberon. They seemed almost like one person in her mind. Even his smile brought back the fear from her meeting with those two men.

"I am Davin, and I will be your instructor in the art of defense."

"Or attack, depending on your point of view." Richard popped up from behind the metal case. Careless blonde hair crowned a lean, tan body. Jaika guessed him to be in his mid-twenties, maybe, she wasn't quite sure. His body definitely projected the proper image of a well-trained fighter, lean and agile, but his smile and that odd sparkle in his blue eyes...maybe he was even younger.

"Of course, I will be assisted by young Richard,"

Davin explained with a hint of agitation.

"My lady," Richard teased, throwing Jaika a quick bow. Something in his manner pleased her immensely, but there was deceit in those eyes. Davin was openly her enemy, but Richard was more difficult to appraise. Jaika made a silent vow to watch him closely.

"Shall we begin?"

"Do I have a choice?" Jaika mocked.

Torin shoved the control box over her shoulder and against her face. "No, you do not."

Jaika had almost forgotten he was still in the room.

Richard hit the side of the metallic box and a door slid open to reveal five thin swords.

"Well." Davin spun on his heel and held out his hand to Richard.

Richard grinned and responded by tossing one of the swords. The handle tumbled in the air to land tight in Davin's outstretched hand. With a zigzagging swoosh, he swept the sword in front of Jaika's face, looking a little like a musketeer. He then turned the handle toward her.

"Richard, I will need a spar."

Quick, light steps and Richard stood beside Davin, sword in hand, blue eyes still gleaming.

"Begin?" Davin prodded, pushing the sword toward Jaika.

Torin grumbled something from his station by the door. Involuntarily, Jaika raised her hand to her new collar and fought the tremble that ran through her body. She took the sword.

Davin shook his head. "Haven't you ever seen a sword before, little girl?" He tilted his head in an arrogant tease.

Jaika tightened her grip and clenched her teeth. She was not about to give in to her fear so quickly.

"Only sticking out of a dead man," she snapped remembering the tapestry in Seela's study room. She had never held a sword but she had held a baseball bat. Maybe they would be alike, at least a little.

Davin's mouth curled in an icy smirk, and he strode behind her, gripping her by the shoulders. He lowered his mouth toward her ear to whisper something dark. She could feel his warm breath prickling her skin.

"Well now, my little Picari." Davin mumbled the name against her neck. The same name Oberon had used.

She jerked away but he dug his fingers deeper into her flesh pulling her back against his body. Shifting his weight, he wrapped his arms completely around her shoulders and gripped her hands against the sword's hilt. "Hold it this way, my little Picari. Don't be afraid."

Jaika felt his breath hot in her ear and wondered what Picari meant. Richard slid into position in front, and their two swords crossed. For an instant Jaika was mesmerized, searching Richard's face, wondering what lay behind those mischievous eyes. Then Davin lunged forward, controlling her arms and the sword with his right hand, pulling her tight against his stomach with his left.

"This way," he whispered. "Thrust and turn."

Their bodies moved in unwilling unison.

Richard's movements were slow and deliberate, meeting Davin's sword with unerring skill. His impish smile was replaced with an uncomfortable silence.

Davin pulled Jaika along in a marionette's dance across the floor, clashing swords, gripping his hand along her stomach and ribs until she could stand no more. In one movement, she twisted in his arms, kicking at his legs with all her strength. Her aim was true, and the sword clattered to the floor. Davin's gasp and staggering step told her she had hit her mark.

Jaika's cheeks glowed red hot as she backed away, hatred rising from within her.

"Does that mean the lesson's over?" Richard asked, unable to hide his pleasure at Jaika's fleeting moment of success.

"Enough games!" Torin growled, stomping across the floor.

"Aaaaaaaaay!" Jaika's stabbing scream shook the mirrored walls, and surprised even Davin. Clutching her neck, sparks flew from between her fingers, and she dropped to her knees.

Torin swung the collar controls in front of Davin's face.

Jaika's vision blurred, but she was sure Torin's face bore the same hatred for her that she felt for Davin.

"If you can't control her, I will!" Torin stormed, glaring down at Davin. He was almost a foot taller and double his weight. He could have easily crushed the swordsman with a single blow.

Davin stroked his chin in thoughtful consideration, completely recovered from Jaika's attack. "Perhaps, I chose her first weapon unwisely." He seemed strangely unaffected by Torin's outburst.

Dismissing her guard with a brush of his hand, Davin pulled a much weakened Jaika from the floor. He ignored the smell of her charred flesh. Visibly shaken, she stumbled over her own feet as Davin drug her to the front stone wall of the training room.

Three silver medallions, chest high, protruded from the white stone. Davin grabbed the middle one, jerking it away from the wall pulling with it a slick, wiry chord. With one quick click, Davin connected the medallion to the back of Jaika's collar, tethering her to the wall.

When Davin released his grip, the wire began to retract, dragging both collar and Jaika back to the stone wall. With a frantic spin, she grabbed the wire, pulling against its strength. It sliced lines deep into the creases of her palms. She dragged her leash and backed away from the wall.

"1, 2, 3," she could hardly speak the words, "4, 5, 6." Twenty paces and Jaika froze, still holding the wire with her bloody hands. She turned to see Davin removing a new weapon from the metal case at the back of the room. His movements were painfully slow like a hunter relishing the final moments of a kill. She watched as Davin lifted what appeared to be a rifle.

With a gentle fffffft from the gun's muzzle, a tiny, glowing orb emerged, no bigger than the end of a pencil. It floated toward the terrified girl. Its light ebbed, and it wafted forward. Jaika began to see tiny crackles and sparks dancing around the outer edge of the sphere. Before the lightning ball could touch her shoulder, Jaika stepped to the side. It traveled past and evaporated a few inches from the stone wall.

"There now, little Picari." Davin mused, gloating at his regained control of the situation. "I knew you would be a quick learner."

He lowered his rifle. "These are burns. They can wound or they can kill. It is completely up to me."

He ran his thumb down his cheek as if considering his options. "What do you think, young Richard? Shall we try again?"

Davin glanced sideways at his apprentice. Richard's childish grin had again vanished, but Davin did not seem to notice. Nor did he wait for an answer.

He raised his weapon and fired. This time the gun recoiled with a kick against his shoulder, hurling a fiery light into Jaika's arm.

She winced and staggered sideways wiping the warm blood from her bicep. The wire tether jerked her a few inches closer to the wall.

"Well," Davin mocked. "I think she needs more practice."

Sporting an excited sneer, he fired again. Jaika jumped as the dime-sized fireball caught her left thigh, slicing her pants and burrowing into the muscle. The burns were getting bigger.

Crack — again...this time the blood ran down her cheek just under her right eye. Two more shots and Davin drove Jaika back against the wall. Blood soiled her chest and neck.

"Enough!" Richard commanded.

Davin instantly responded with a cautioning glare, and Richard's eyes softened. He seemed to think better of his anger...

"She's out of range now," Richard soothed, his grin returning. "No need to waste any more burns."

"They are only practice rounds," Davin explained.

"The shots won't kill. Isn't that right, Jaika?"

She couldn't speak. She just stared at the blood on her hands and the blood that ran down her leg onto her left boot.

Just for fun, Davin laughed and fired two more shots. Each burn missed its mark to flicker and explode beside her face.

Jaika fainted, still hanging from the tether.

Levek

"Ughhhhhh," Jaika moaned and strained to open her eyes.

A gentle hum washed over her skin and feather light touches danced across her body sending a ticklish shiver across her back.

"Lie still, my little one." A gentle voice soothed and sang. "The pain will soon be gone." The words hypnotized, almost magical, wrapping Jaika in a lulling blanket of warmth.

"Where...," she tried to speak but could not find the words. The world felt very far away and very unimportant.

"You must not speak little one." The singing words came again. "Save your strength."

What strength, thought Jaika. She could barely move. Her little finger weighed a million pounds. She

131

drifted in and out of a sea of unconsciousness. The lullaby hum was the only sound that mattered.

Feathery caresses flitted around her neck then continued along her chest to settle on her left thigh. The burning sensation there dissipated and then completely vanished. True to the singing words of her unknown companion, her pain began to fade. In that truth, Jaika found the strength to open her eyes.

Her surroundings were blurry at best. She could see the feathery touches that took away the pain came from long ropes that danced and flew above her. Jaika squinted to find their point of origin. A lump formed in her throat as she realized the ropes were not ropes at all but arms — tentacle like arms — thin, tubular arms weaving across her body with skill and purpose. She felt their silken warmth as each arm brushed across her wounds working their healing magic.

"Ahhh," it crooned. "You are already feeling better."

The rhythmic words and the soothing hum came from a gnome-like man. No, now he was taller. Jaika watched as he manipulated his height as best fit his need. Rising to reach across her body and then dropping again to gnome size. Humming...always humming.

"I am Levek, my little one. Do not be afraid."

Jaika stared into his enormous green eyes, much too big for his face. Warm, leafy green eyes. Eyes that comforted and soothed. Eyes surrounded by a child's face, and yet he seemed wise beyond years. Round bald head, pale skin. Even as he returned her fear with a smile, he sang.

"I am almost finished. Only one more place to reach." A single arm brushed her cheek as the other three worked undisturbed. Delicate painter's strokes, but Jaika got the feeling those arms could be quite powerful if the need arose.

"Where am I?" Jaika's voice cracked with the question.

"This is where you will live now, little one. Richard carried you here after Davin..."

Levek's eyes clouded and he rose to his full height. Jaika could feel the beginning of anger as he towered over her.

Davin, yes Davin, she remembered. Vivid, painful images of her training session tore into her thoughts. Davin...the gun...and Richard. Levek said Richard had carried her here. Was every training session going to be this painful? And what was she being trained for?

Jaika watched Levek move away. He wore a loose fitting, cottony-white tunic, making it difficult to see any form to his torso. He swayed as he walked, scooping up a black bag with one of his many arms. Jaika tried to imagine what kind of strange thin body might hide beneath the layers of white.

"Rest now, little one," he sang as he walked. "You will need all of your strength."

A heavy wooden door opened to free him, and Jaika heard the jingle of keys. Torin was nearby.

Dreamily, she watched the door close and took one long look at the empty room around her. The walls shone with light. At least she was not in the underground level anymore... shiny was good. Not underground... Levek... Richard... for the second time today, Jaika lost consciousness.

Map

"Good morning, little Picari," Oberon's words were icy slick. He used that name again – just like Davin.

Jaika sat motionless on the small cot in her latest prison. The same room where Levek had mended her wounds. Unlike the old room, this one was well lit by a pair of yellow potted glowers. The walls were still bare and windowless, but there was no mistaking their shine. A small, open bath held personal items such as soap and a towel, but no privacy, and nothing sharp or pointy.

Oberon slipped into the room through the heavy door. His cloak rippling behind him. Jaika tried to look at his face, but she could not take her eyes off the blue pendant that dangled from his neck.

"Picari. Why do you call me that?" Jaika snapped, staring at the dark-haired man. The same man who had stood beside Kaleus. The same man who had kissed her neck... He wasn't her friend. She knew that much.

"You don't remember your father, do you?" Oberon ignored her question. "He was a king you know." He moved closer as he spoke.

Jaika studied the pendant. It was full of cracks and tiny holes, and one edge was missing altogether. There was some sort of writing on the front but the symbols were worn and unfamiliar. She pulled her feet underneath her to sit up on her knees, mesmerized by the pendant but wanting to know more about her father. Although she wasn't sure she could believe anything this man said.

"He was once the greatest king on Regar." He tilted his head to study her reactions.

"So... now Kaleus is... the greatest?" Jaika tested.

"He believes so," Oberon grasped his pendant. "I let him believe so. I keep him strong and apathetic." He touched his medallion. "So really...that makes me the greatest king."

Jaika waited for something to happen.

"The people believe they serve Kaleus, when, in fact, it is me they serve."

"And my father serves you too?" Jaika murmured and bit at the quiver in her lower lip.

"No, he has been destroyed." He stated this truth in a matter-of-fact way, never breaking his stare, never twitching a muscle.

Jaika's stomach tightened. She felt hollow... empty... and she slid from the cot to stand. "If he is gone, then I have nothing to lose," she challenged, daring him to take action, even as her heart withered and failed.

His only response was a muffled laugh. "Torin is busy with other matters. I, Oberon, will be your escort today." He swept his arm toward the open door and initiated a bow. In his hand he held the metal box Torin had carried to activate her collar.

"I can hardly wait," Jaika whispered. She moved toward the door, careful not to walk too close to Oberon.

I must be moving up she thought as they walked. No dank, stale air or dirt floors. Her new cell must be on a higher level of the castle. The stone walls sparkled, and Jaika even saw a window here and there as they walked together down the hallway. Her stomach knotted as she realized they were walking back to the same training room as yesterday. She wondered if Davin would be there, and if he would have his gun.

They stopped in front of the wooden door that bore the emblem of the crossed swords. Oberon pushed the door to hold it open for her, pretending to have manners.

There was Davin, standing in the middle of the room studying a large map which lay at his feet. The map was at least four feet across and looked like a sheet taken from one of Mattie's beds. Again he was dressed in black causing Jaika to wonder if Kaleus kept everyone in black just to make his fancy clothes look better.

As Jaika approached, she could see the map more clearly. A floor plan she guessed by its many straight lines and right angles.

"Sit," Davin commanded and pointed to the far side of the map directly across from him.

Jaika wanted to yell 'I am not a dog' but reconsidered. She glanced over her shoulder at Oberon. His mood had not softened the least bit, and she found herself missing Torin. He would at least feel some remorse if he killed her, maybe. Oberon, on the other hand, hated everything and everyone. A man who could commit murder and then sit down to a nice lunch.

"Sit," Davin repeated with an impatient huff.

Jaika slipped to the floor to sit crossed-legged with her chin in her hand. Her muscles showed no painful reminders of yesterday's training which meant she could be brought close to death on a daily basis and then right back to life for more torture. Still, she could not help but smile at Levek's handiwork.

"You are looking at the inside of a castle," Davin instructed.

"This one?" Jaika questioned.

"No. Now be still and listen."

"It is the castle of a murderer." Both Davin and Jaika jumped at Oberon's words. "The man who killed your father."

A strange look of understanding passed between the two men. "Please continue, Master Davin. I did not mean to interrupt."

He apologized but Jaika didn't think he was really sorry.

"As I was saying," Davin's arrogance returned, "This solid line represents the back wall of a castle." He pointed. "There are several small buildings located just below the wall. Put your hand on one."

Jaika pointed to the middle building.

"That is a merchant's tent," Davin continued. "On either side is a small wooden shack. These also house merchants. The last... no... move your hand over... the last shape is a prophetess. She tells of the future under a dismal brown tarp. Are you listening?"

"Am I going to have my fortune told?" Jaika watched Davin from under her eyelashes.

"Your future is no mystery, my dear." Oberon cautioned from behind her. "I see only pain and death."

Jaika refused to look back. "This is the fortune teller's tent, right?" She moved her hand to the last square shape and waited.

"Yes," Davin nodded. "There are also taverns further out from her tent. The castle walls are easily accessible from there."

"We are going there?" Jaika mused, not sure if it was a good thing or a bad.

"You are," Oberon answered. "I am giving you a chance for vengeance – a chance to kill the man that killed your father."

"What if I don't want to kill him?" Jaika had that same sinking feeling as when she saw the sand at the edge of the garden. When she had worked so hard to escape from Torin only to find there was no place to go.

"Did you know that Seela has a son?" Oberon had watched Jaika with Seela. He knew they had developed the beginning of a friendship that he could exploit.

Jaika swallowed hard and chose her words carefully. "Does he live in the castle?"

"No, you Bartok, he works in the mines!" Davin snapped.

Oberon's glare silenced Davin's outburst. Whatever Oberon was up to, Davin did not seem to be in on the plan.

"Davin is right," he continued. "Her son works in the mines... the crystal mines. The crystals that provide fuel for our world."

Jaika watched as Oberon walked around the edge of the map. He looked at the ceiling and gestured upward in a nobody-understands-me sort of way. "Jaika, my Jaika. Our world cannot survive without crystals. We cook our food, heat our rooms, and even power our weapons with crystals." He turned toward his captive audience. "You must understand."

Jaika nodded, not sure what else to do.

"The mines are a dangerous place, my little Picari. Accidents happen there so often. So many could lose their lives."

Jaika held her breath.

"Seela has a son there." Davin continued, "Torin's wife... even Davin has given up his family."

If Torin and Seela had not already explained, Jaika would have seen this as just another one of Oberon's lies. But she knew it must be the truth. So many people...

"Of course, they are strangers to you. You do not care what happens to them."

She felt like a rat trapped in a maze except there was no cheese at the center, only death for someone. "1, 2, 3..." she whispered, "one step at a time." She raised her voice. "I don't want anyone to die."

"Of course not. Only those who deserve to die." Oberon knew his threat had hit its mark. She would not risk the lives of the workers in the mines. "I think it is time to continue our lesson."

Davin nodded measuring Oberon's warning. He was right. The city could not survive without the crystals, but killing workers would limit production. He smiled softly. Of course, there were always more workers to be found, in other cities.

"Oberon is right. You have much to learn. Show me where the prophetess lives. Do you remember?"

Jaika pointed to the symbol, thinking about Seela and her son.

"Now the castle wall. Find the towers... Do you see the symbol for guards?"

The lesson continued until Davin grew weary and bored. With a militant spin, he headed to the back of the room and the metallic cabinet. From its insides, he pulled a weapon and a gray tablet. Jaika tightened her jaw as she recognized the gun from yesterday's session. Pulling her knees up, she moved to stand only to be shoved back to the ground by a fiery grip to her shoulder.

"Be patient, my dear," Oberon soothed. "Death will come soon enough."

She could still feel his fingers digging into her shoulder when Davin laid the gun beside the map and dropped the gray tablet with a black stick directly in front of her. Then he kicked the map to one side.

"Draw it." Davin snapped. "Draw all you have learned."

Jaika stared at the gun and the wrinkled mess that had been a map. She shivered with the memory of the burning bullets fired into her leg and chest and the wire that had choked and cut into her neck. So she drew. Digging into the tablet with the writing stick, she drew.

Hope

Jaika did not see Oberon the next day. In fact, it would be quite some time until they met again. Torin returned to his vigil, and each day progressed with dull repetition. Each morning Davin drilled her on the map and each afternoon Richard joined them for weapons practice. The trainings were harsh and Levek was a constant visitor to Jaika's cell. His hypnotic song was almost a permanent sound in Jaika's ear. She would already be dead from Davin's games if not for Levek's skills.

This morning's lesson, however, would be different. Davin was away with Kaleus or Oberon, Jaika didn't really care where, so Richard would be her only instructor. Torin watched from his usual post by the training room entrance while Richard fitted Jaika with a blindfold.

"Once you enter the castle, there will be no light. Not a torch... not a glower."

Holding her shoulders, Richard guided the now blind Jaika to a marked starting point. Before her lay two parallel lines representing an imaginary hallway.

"You have just entered the hidden door in the back wall of the castle." He slipped his hands from her shoulders. "Which way?"

"Forward, of course." Jaika snickered and took a step. To her surprise, her foot stamped hard to the ground. Without her vision, her steps were teetering and unsure. She took a second, more cautious step.

"Count Jaika. How many steps?"

"4," she hesitated, "no 5, 6." Jaika crumpled to the floor, her balance spinning and lost.

"Crawl if you have to. Keep going forward."

"9... 10," Jaika crawled forward. "13... 14"

"Keep going," Richard ordered. She could hear his voice off to the right.

"40, 41," Jaika yelled. "The hallway ends here." With a quick tug, the blindfold fell from her eyes. To her amazement, she was completely off course. She had traveled at least twenty feet in the wrong direction.

Richard chuckled. "At least inside the castle you will run into the wall."

Jaika blew out her breath. "Why do I want to go into this stupid castle anyway?" She sat on the cold floor, defeated.

"It is important. That is all I can tell you... now." Richard's smile was gone and his forehead creased with worry. He threw a cautious glance across his shoulder as if he had heard an unidentified noise, and Jaika could not help but wonder if someone, unseen, was watching or listening.

"Did the ruler of this castle really kill my father?" Jaika offered the question, deathly afraid of its answer.

"Who told you that?" He guarded his expression as he spoke, but Jaika caught his bewilderment.

"Oberon," Jaika tested, "Oberon and Davin."

Richard cut his eyes away seemingly to search for an answer.

"They lied didn't they?" But Jaika already knew the answer. So much of this world was built on lies.

"It's complicated." Richard explained, flashing Jaika an almost pleading look, but it was gone in a heartbeat.

"Let's try it again," Richard's smile returned as if the conversation had never happened. "Shall we?"

Davin's absence changed the very air in the room. When Richard smiled, Jaika was swept up in his charm. His Cheshire cat grin and child-like innocence took over his every feature, and she found herself wanting to learn... to be successful just to please him.

She stood and walked back to the beginning of the imaginary hallway.

"Don't forget your eyes," Richard scolded playfully, tossing her the blindfold.

She met his gaze as she reached for the cloth... those joyous eyes. He watched her with such caution as though he held a world of secrets he longed to share. Secrets she ached to know. Feeling his eyes on her nurtured a most precious sensation — hope. Maybe her father was still alive. Richard knew and he would tell her someday, when he could. Maybe he would even help her escape this awful place.

"Now forward, Jaika. Slowly this time. Lead with your toes," Richard guided.

One, two, three steps. She focused only on his voice.

"Keep going."

She could hear his strength, his... concern. Yes, that was what she heard. His concern for her safety. Images of their first training session returned. Davin with the burn rifle and Richard commanding him to stop.

"18, 19... you can do it."

Why does he care about my safety?

"22," Richard's voice rose and Jaika fell to the ground. "22 steps. Halfway!"

Jaika's head spun and her knees ached from the fall. "Halfway," she murmured, "great, just great." Her fingers dug at the blindfold.

"Jaika." Richards's voice soft from behind her. "I know... I know. Do it again."

If he is concerned for my safety, why doesn't he take me out of here, Jaika thought, stifling the urge to yell. Tell me! Tell me everything! Why am I here? Who is my father? Why am I walking this stupid hallway? But she didn't yell, she just stood to make another try.

#

Jaika ate her lunch portion in silence, cross-legged on the training room floor. Torin ate as well, but he sat by the door to block her only possible escape. She could see him watching her in the mirror. He would look away only to retrieve a bite of food from his plate. She thought about the first time they met. When he had brought her through the wall of light. The day she had tried to escape, he never hit her. He had wanted to, oh how he had wanted to, but something stopped him.

She took a deep breath and summoned her sweetest voice. "Please tell me about your wife." Jaika watched an expression of shock fire across the guard's face. "Where is Mara now?"

Torin swallowed his last bite of bread, but it seemed to stick in his throat at the thought of his wife. "Mara," he whispered her name with such grief, Jaika thought for a moment he might even shed a tear. "My Mara still works in the crystal mines."

Jaika waited for him to say something else. The silence fell across them – a thick, sticky silence. Torin was not ready to answer questions.

"How long?" Jaika met his gaze in the mirror. His eyes soft with memories.

"Twenty-seven crossings of the yellow moon," he sighed, "and three suns."

Moon cycles thought Jaika. On Earth the moon cycled about once a month. Did he mean 27 months or 27 days? Had Mara been gone over two years? "And you work for Kaleus?"

The sadness in his eyes instantly disappeared and a bitter hatred hardened his face. "I work to keep Mara alive!" Torin stood but would not meet her eyes.

Jaika could see his chest heave with each breath.

"That is what we *all* do." Torin glared toward the mirror. "Except your teachers. They..." Torin glanced across his shoulder much like Richard had done in the morning lesson. "Eat!" Torin commanded, then sat back down beside his plate. There would be no more questions answered.

Jaika watched him push the food around on his plate. Her thoughts were filled with the mystery of Mara. Where were these crystal mines? And who was in there? Torin had said 'all', 'that is what we all do.' How many others had loved ones in the mines?

Richard soon returned for afternoon weapons practice. He whistled an odd tune as he pulled two swords from the metal storage unit at the back of the room. Light danced along each shaft to sparkle again on the mirrored wall.

"Are you ready?" Richard grinned, pushing the sword's handle toward his student.

He knows full well I am not ready. Why does he ask, Jaika mused? *And what reason does he have to be so happy?* Jaika gripped the sword in her right hand but let it trail against the floor.

"Why?" Jaika sighed, staring at the sword tip on the ground. "I don't want to fight anyone. Why do I have to learn?"

Richard studied her weary posture. There were so many things to tell her, but he had no answers to this question. He knew Kaleus and Oberon would use Jaika to fulfill the prophecy. He just wasn't sure how.

"Kaleus ordered your training. That's enough. No more questions," Richard explained.

"It's not enough," Jaika sighed but raised her sword anyway. She couldn't help but feel angry toward Richard... toward Richard, Davin, Kaleus, Torin... toward everyone on Regar.

She drew to her full height and whip-cracked her sword in the air, flashing it in front of Richard's face. "Take your best shot," Jaika challenged.

Richard took up the gauntlet without hesitation, his impish pleasure danced across his grinning face. "You are not ready for my best shot, my lady," he teased.

His sword met hers with a clash and he began to drive forward. Slice, thrust, step – they danced together. Jaika watched the tilt of his shoulders to anticipate his attack just as he had taught her. She could see his weight shift as he maneuvered toward her left. Each slice of his weapon readily met with resistance from hers.

"You can do better than that!" Jaika called, ducking a wide swing of her opponent's sword.

His eyes sparkled with her taunt, as he moved in rhythm, allowing Jaika to match his pace but always staying one step ahead. She had learned a great deal, but he was still the teacher.

Their swords met just above the floor and Jaika did the one thing she had been warned never to do. She made full eye contact with her opponent. Never meet their eyes, Davin had preached. They are only the enemy until you look into their eyes, then they become a living, breathing creature.

"Who is my father?" The words whispered from her lips, yet they sounded like thunder in her ears.

Richard froze, their swords still crossed.

Jaika took a step backward to release the tension from the swords. Instinct took over rational thought and Richard reacted. He swung his weapon upward to defend against a strike that never came. He was caught off balance and sliced deep into Jaika's shoulder. A sharp cry of pain, a wild swing, and Jaika opened a gash in Richard's tunic — horizontal, chest level. His tunic hung open almost to his stomach revealing a tiny thread of blood.

He staggered backward. His sword dragging along the ground. His eyes wide in disbelief. "Your arm," he lamented, "forgive me."

Jaika shuddered, staring at the bloody wound across her teacher's chest. In an unexpected clatter, her sword dropped to the training room floor and her right hand flew to cover her own wound. Her shoulder burning with the movement.

Richard's sword joined Jaika's on the ground. His arm reached to the back of his neck to pull his shredded tunic up over his head. Using his shirt as a bandage, he moved to wipe the blood from Jaika's shoulder. She stared into his worried face, feeling him push her hand away to cover her wound with his shirt.

"Does it hurt?" Richard questioned as he studied the baffled look on the girl's face.

She could only shake her head yes and stare. Her eyes drifted across his face, his strong compassionate face, along his neck and down to the line of blood across his chest. His body hard and chiseled with years of battle training. Then Jaika caught her breath and stepped away. Her eyes fixed on the soldier's chest. Below the bloody line she had cut lay the remains of another wound. A ragged diagonal scar running the full length of his chest. She could hear the echoes of rushing water and wood cracking.

Jaika drew an audible, quivering breath. "Ree?" She whispered. Her eyes reached deep into his soul.

In a step, he was again in front of her. His fingers dug into her arm and he pulled her, almost lifted her from the ground.

Jaika winced from his grip and twisted to escape but not before she saw the wild look on his face. He released her and turned away, closing his eyes and scolding himself for his carelessness, for hurting her.

Torin intervened, destroying any further questions. "I will take the girl to Levek to be repaired."

His words made Jaika feel like a broken piece of furniture.

"Maybe you should go too." Torin nodded at Richard's bloody chest but showed no concern at the ragged scar beneath it nor any indication that Richard's behavior was anything but normal.

"Take her," Richard snarled.

Jaika was led away like a wounded animal. She could feel Richard's eyes watching her as she walked with Torin to the doorway. Their eyes met for an instant in the mirrored wall and she knew he remembered. The bridge, the water, the scar, the fear... everything was in his eyes in the moment they shared in the glass.

Assassin

The next morning, it was not Torin's hands that carried Jaika's usual breakfast. Instead Davin held the sparsely set tray. Bread and fruit served with a smile; a self-righteous, arrogant smile – void of happiness, filled with only the primitive satisfaction of an animal before it feeds.

"Eat up, my little Picari. We will be leaving soon. Today you will complete your training."

Jaika desperately wanted to ask where they were going, but she wasn't about to give Davin that satisfaction. In her heart, she already knew. She knew they were going to another man's home. The home of a king. A place where she would have to kill a man she had never met to save people she had never met. She had tried desperately to come up with a plan to avoid the whole situation. If given a chance, only a tiny chance, she would run. If Richard or Davin killed her trying to escape, she would never have to decide who lives or dies.

So she ate.

Davin watched as she ate, lounging against the wall, urging her to completion with his eyes. Jaika defied him in the only way possible at the moment. She chewed each morsel slowly, taking tiny, delicate bites, keeping them on her tongue while enjoying Davin's displeasure.

When he could tolerate her complacency no more, he kicked the tray to the wall and ordered her to follow. Together, they walked down the endless stone hallways without windows to a door, a new door that looked very much like every other door she had entered since her arrival at Kaleus's castle.

Davin opened the door and pushed Jaika inside. "Get dressed," he barked, and closed the door behind her. A dull, heavy click, and she was alone.

This room was larger than her prison cell but the air smelled of dust and loneliness. The walls were covered with black wood that looked as though they would leave splinters in your fingers if you touched them. All across the walls stood dark, heavy cabinets, with bolted doors and chained locks. The top doors of each cabinet were clear, like glass, but much thicker. She doubted if any man could shatter them. Her eyes did not linger on the strength of the glass but what lay beyond it, inside the cabinets.

Weapons...

Swords of every thickness, shields polished to an eerie shine, helmets, axes, and pieces of what could have been armor straight from Camelot. At the end of the room, in front of the most lethal weapons, were her clothes, folded neatly in front of the cabinet doors. She moved toward them unable to take her eyes from the barbed metal behind the glass. Two foot rods with hooks and razors on the top edges lay in stacks against the back wall of the cabinet. Stringy whips hung above them, dangling, painful blades with twisted iron at the ends. Jaika could almost see the prisoners being beaten with those horrible creations, almost hear their screams.

Davin was warning her to behave. Without speaking a word, he had issued the gravest of ultimatums, warning her of what he was capable of doing. For a split second, she considered what damage she could do to Davin with one of those weapons, and her heart almost stopped.

She dressed there, in front of the glass. Staring at the blades, and allowing Davin's warning to weave through her bones much like the laces in her boots. He had brought her a soldier's uniform. Black pants, black tunic, but her boots were soft soled, light and limber, a woman's boots for walking unheard — not the heavy steel-toed boots that Davin wore.

"Where are you taking me?" Jaika whispered to the walls, then turned to see if anyone had heard. She mentally scolded herself for letting Davin get the best of her. Of course there was no one there. Jaika didn't want to go with Davin, but she didn't want to stay here either, alone with these memories of death.

In the hallway, she found Davin waiting. He raised his eyebrow and sneered looking through her as if he knew everything she'd been thinking inside the room of weapons.

"I'm ready," Jaika offered trying to look unaffected by what she'd seen.

"I doubt that," he grumbled then led her away.

Jaika looked down at her feet as they walked. *1, 2, 3 steps.* Counting kept her busy, kept her from worrying. Someone had told her that, once, somewhere...

"Keep up, Picari," Davin barked opening yet another wooden door.

Jaika gave out a tiny gasp at the sunlight that exploded into the hallway. This door was different than the others. This door led outside.

The minute she cleared the doorway the aroma of the garden lifted her spirits. The sunlight warmed her skin making her believe for a heartbeat that everything would be all right. That there was still goodness in the universe and it would find her somehow. On this horrible, lonely, planet, she could still find hope.

Beyond the garden, outside the viney blossoms and flowering fruit trees, Richard waited. His clothes were the same tawny color as the empty sands beyond him. His arm stretched out to hold the reins of three very bored saktars, but his eyes were on Jaika.

Not horses, Jaika thought, but almost. Ugly, flat feet, camel's feet, a saktar was a wide horse with camel's feet. She found the thought amusing right along with the idea of riding one. Just like the garden blossomed, her amusement turned into hope, hope that they were leaving this place. And for the second time today, her spirits rose with possibilities.

"Are the supplies ready?" Davin snapped, taking the reins from Richard.

Davin's sharp words did nothing to daunt Richard's good nature. "Everything is as you ordered," Richard responded, not looking nearly as submissive as his answer. He motioned to the bundles strapped behind the saddles of each saktar. Then he turned to Jaika and held out his hand in assistance. "Time to get aboard," he announced.

She studied his face for any sign of remembrance. She was sure he was the man from her dreams, the man on the bridge, but here, with Davin watching, he would give her nothing.

"The middle one's yours," Richard nodded, amused by her hesitation.

She had ridden a horse twice in her life, so she knew she could manage a saddle, at least the getting-on part. As she swung her body upward into the saddle, her leg hit the provisions tied to the saktar's back. Too many provisions for a short trip, she thought, feeling the saktar shifting beneath her weight. She turned her head to look out at the endless sand, her mouth already dry. Then she turned back to see Richard and Davin swing themselves on their saktars with the ease of taking a breath.

"Come," Davin commanded. He turned his mount and rode away knowing Jaika had little choice in the matter.

Her saktar followed Davin even though no one had told it to do so. Jaika certainly had not moved. Her heart dropped a little at this creature's blind obedience. Even the animals of this planet felt the futility of rebellion. Richard fell in behind, single file, and for a minute Jaika entertained the idea of escape. She had provisions and a means of transportation, but there was no place to go. Mountains silhouetted the horizon to her right, but it would take days to get there. Davin would surely catch her. So, she had no other choice but to ride wherever her saktar would take her... wherever Davin led.

#

The days were hot and the air breathless. The mountains sizzled in the distance leaving no wind to dry their sweat-soaked skin. Richard gave Jaika a greasy lotion to rub on her face and neck, and on her hands. It turned her skin a dirty brown, but Richard said it would block out the sun. He also said it would keep her cooler, but he must have lied. She didn't think it was possible to be any hotter. Sometimes she covered her head with an extra tunic, but the heat always fought its way through. Their saktars just seemed annoyed.

Above them, impervious to the temperature, in the cloudless, sunbaked sky, the Breen followed. Winged, Pterodactyl-looking creatures, large enough to carry her away but easily fought off by a grown man. That is, if they attacked one at a time. The pack that followed them had twelve members, circling buzzard-like in the sky, always just ahead or just behind. They never came low enough for a really good look. Some were larger than others; some cat sized, some more like lions. She wasn't sure if the smaller birds were young ones or females or maybe both. There were always two stragglers at the back of the group. These birds seemed to have trouble just flying much less keeping up. Maybe they were the entertainment for the large birds.

"Birds," she whispered. There were no birds like these in Mattie's neighborhood but no other word seemed to fit.

Davin said they usually attacked the injured or dying. They would steal a man's water and provisions and eventually devour the whole man. Richard's eyes sparkled at Davin's stories of the Breen and their ruthlessness causing Jaika to wonder if his words were meant only to keep her from trying to escape. True or not, she kept a constant watch on the Breen just to be safe.

As they journeyed, the night brought the only true relief. At the end of each day, as the sun disappeared, it mercifully carried the heat right along with it. The air would cool to a breathable temperature, the Breen would disappear, and the three of them would sleep beneath the stars.

Jaika would lie on her pallet looking up at the red moon and the yellow. The yellow moon was so much smaller. Its light pale and weak as though it took every ounce of its strength to glow. The red moon was different. Blood red, almost hot; it held the strength of an army, and yet its presence was oddly comforting. Surely as a child, she must have loved this moon, but from where did she see it? Did she stand at the gates of Kaleus's castle or atop its walls to view this crimson orb, or somewhere else? Somewhere... she couldn't remember.

Each day followed as the one before. Three saktars trudged through the endless sands, unrelenting heat pushing them back, hazy mountains in the distance, and the ever-vigilant Breen. Then on the fifth day, the landscape began to change, almost imperceptibly at first. Here and there the sand would be broken with a pebble or some dry grass. A patch of sand that looked like cracking mud hinted at water that might lie beneath the ground. As they continued, those pebbles became rocks.

The rocks grew into gray boulders. The mountains were moving closer, or maybe Davin's course was simply turning. She couldn't be sure either way. It was just too hot to think clearly.

The changing scenery was not as worrisome as their followers. As the terrain shifted, the Breen closed their distance, circling tighter, and dropping closer to the three weary saktars, and closer to Jaika.

That night the men slept in shifts, hidden among the rocks to better study the night. Davin kept watch until the yellow moon rose beside the red, high amid the star- peppered sky. Then Richard took his turn at guard. Jaika felt like she never slept at all, tossing and turning, always listening for the sound of wings.

At dawn, the sun brought the heat and a new sound. Curtains fluttering in the wind, at least that's what it sounded like to Jaika. For a second, she could see Mattie and her lace curtains blowing in the breeze. Softly at first, swaying in the distance, then beating against the walls as the wind rose driving the sleep from her eyes.

The dream vanished, and Jaika was once again on the rocky sand. Just Jaika, Richard, Davin and the Breen. There were no curtains, only wings, ragged, leathery wings, flailing at the air.

Richard's rough hand caught Jaika's arm and dragged her body into the rocks. He shoved her between twin boulders. She didn't even feel the scratches the rocks cut into her hands.

"Stay down!" He yelled into her face, as if she had any other plans. His gun slid from his hip. "Aim for the leader!" He shouted into the air, firing skyward but hitting nothing.

"I know," Davin answered, half yelling half commanding. "I taught you that, whelp, remember?"

The Breen dove into the rocks. Their razor-sharp claws cut slices into the boulders that stood between them and Jaika. She watched them circling and diving. How could anyone possibly find a leader among all those wings? Coarse, leathery wings that popped like canvas sails in the wind. Birds she had called them; birds that were ready to kill, and she had no weapon.

Richard fired again into the gathering storm of Breen. Their flight became erratic, darting, insect like, revealing only flashes of wings and eyes. Those eyes filled with hatred when they dove; red, iridescent eyes, never blinking, never closing, only watching their mark.

Richard continued firing, wounding one of the smaller birds. It fled the group to disappear into the morning sky. Davin growled in pain as a set of Breen claws tore into him, leaving his tunic shredded and bloody at the shoulder.

The attack slowed for a moment. Like the tide, the Breen withdrew to assess their wounded and reset their positions. Jaika lifted her head above the rocks just high enough to watch their retreat, but not too high. And, that's when she saw them. At the edge of their camp lay two dead Breen. The two small stragglers that had flown always behind the others — not much larger than kittens —lifeless kittens. Their bodies had been cut from end to end. Their heads severed and tossed aside.

"When did...," Jaika stammered, the nausea rising in her throat. "They're so small..."

Richard had relaxed among the rocks and now followed her gaze to the butchered bodies. "Davin! You Bartok!"

Davin stared at Richard and then stood among the rocks, leaning against a tall boulder.

"You brought them down on us!" Richard snarled. "You know they were just looking for food!"

"That's why they are so angry," Jaika groaned, shaking her head. "How could you? They were so small."

Davin shrugged. "No one cares. They are worthless animals..." He bristled as he spoke, "They were trying to kill us! Have you forgotten that?"

"You killed first," Jaika offered. Deep in her heart she knew that Davin could kill her just as easily as the tiny Breen. She was just as worthless in his eyes.

"They are coming back!" Richard barked.

"Can't we just hide?" Suddenly Jaika didn't want to kill any more birds. She stared at Davin as if the power of her thoughts might be enough to make him change his mind.

"How dare you look at me with such arrogance! I will not be questioned?" Davin planted his feet and swung his weapon toward the sky and the oncoming birds. He released all of his anger into the spiraling Breen. "I will kill as I please..."

The rhythm of his gunfire pounded against Jaika's ears. "1, 2, 3..." she counted without meaning to, "4, 5, 6."

The Breen shrieked louder than before. Jaika covered her ears and wiggled a little deeper into the rocks as the pounding of wings began again. The air smelled like charred meat. She wanted it to be the gun and not the burning flesh of the Breen.

One of Davin's blasts struck its mark, wounding one of the largest Breen. A bone-piercing shriek shattered the swarm and scattered them in all directions. The bird struggled to stay airborne. His body sunk closer to the sand as his injured wings were no longer able to hold his weight. The bird flailed at the air, howling in pain like fingernails drug across a chalkboard. Jaika felt the sting of his pain-wracked screams and could bear no more.

"Stop!" she screamed. "You'll kill all of them! Stop!" Her words echoed against the rocks and rose above the cries of the Breen.

Davin stood frozen. His body trembled with anger. Jaika waited for him to turn, to run toward her. She waited for the pounding of his fists against her face. But he only shot her a murderous glare and walked away – away from the safety of the rocks and into the open sand.

The Breen withdrew to the tallest rocks perching like clothespins on Mattie's line in the backyard. The injured bird lay fluttering on the sand, 100 yards out from the rocks, unprotected. It would stand on wobbly legs, unfurl its blood-soaked wings to rise and then settle back to the sand. The dark wings were covered with a green, shiny goo that Jaika knew must be blood. The bird had a long way to go before death, but he wasn't able to fly away just yet.

Davin started walking toward the wounded animal with clear intentions to destroy it. Jaika could sense the weariness in both the Breen and Davin, but more than that was the feeling of hopelessness that covered them all.

"1, 2, 3..." Jaika jumped from her hiding spot among the rocks. "4, 5, 6..." she ran. She ran toward Davin, toward the open sand, and toward the Breen. Her heart felt like it would explode at any minute. The Breen might kill her, or maybe Davin would do it for them. But she wanted it all to stop. Even if she died today this journey would be over, and she wouldn't have to be afraid any longer... and she wouldn't have to kill anyone.

Her feet carried her past Davin and out into the open just in front of the now still Breen. Davin stopped, surprised at what was happening, frozen with indecision.

Richard had not moved since seeing the Breen fall to the ground. Like a scene in a play, he had watched the actors present their lines and move about the stage. But he knew the dark things that Davin was capable of carrying out. He had seen firsthand the heartlessness of this man, and now, both the Breen and Jaika would know too if he did nothing.

"Whoa, that was a great shot," Richard tried to work his charm. "I don't think that Breen knew what hit him." He walked as he spoke, moving toward Davin and the sweet spot between him and Jaika.

The air shook around Davin as Richard closed the distance. "I think we should pack it up and keep moving toward the castle. We still have a day's journey ahead, as long as the path through the rocks is not blocked." He could see Davin considering his options, and he hoped killing Jaika wasn't one of them.

Richard walked past Davin well beyond the reach of his fist. He didn't want a fight if he could avoid it. As he moved closer to Jaika, he turned to face his partner. "We still have a mission to complete, right? The mission comes first?"

Davin did not respond, and Richard wondered if his anger had completely blocked his ability to reason. "I don't want to be the one to explain to Kaleus that we failed because of a lousy Breen." He could see a shudder run through Davin at the mention of Kaleus. "And, we need the girl for the mission."

Jaika stared at Richard's broad shoulders, numb from the fear and weariness that painted her body. They waited for what seemed like a million years before Davin moved. In slow motion, he turned and started back into the camp. Davin picked up a canvas bag and started stuffing equipment inside. Richard followed without looking back at Jaika. She knew they were both furious with her, and that she was only alive because of the mission.

She turned to look at the injured Breen sitting on the sand. His eyes were not as red as she remembered. He didn't look invincible or vicious. He just looked weary and maybe a little grateful. His beak swung wide as he lowered his head in what Jaika would choose to believe was a thank you. She stood and started back to camp watching the rest of the Breen above her and hoping the path through the rocks would be closed.

A day's ride to the castle, Richard had said. A day's ride and then she would have to decide who would live and who would die.

Escape

The Breen no longer followed them through the rocks. The pass was open and they arrived at the city by the end of the day, just as Richard had predicted. Davin guided them to the edge of town avoiding people who might ask questions or slow them down. In the darkness, they stopped at a shabby looking wooden building. There were stables at the side, and the sign above the door seemed to indicate a hotel of some kind, though Jaika couldn't understand all of the words.

Jaika watched her companions dismount. They argued and then Richard went inside. In a few minutes, he came out leading a round faced woman with her hair pulled back in a tight bun. If Mattie had been there, this could easily have been a dull-red brick building with Mrs. Box tending to lost souls in her mission house. She hoped the bread would taste as good as it did that first night she spent with Inita, their first night in a new world.

Jaika

Richard motioned for Jaika to dismount. A man took their saktars to the stables beside the inn and then they went inside. Jaika was immediately bathed in the smell of alcohol and sweat and she hoped she did not smell the same way. The voices were loud and a man played what looked like a guitar from a corner chair, though the tones were much higher pitched. The tables resembled the outdoor picnic tables Jaika had seen at the parks by Mattie's house. Pieces of rough wood with legs that made a giant 'X'. She didn't smell any bread, but a young girl brought them some kind of soup with a bowl of lumpy crackers. Salty chunks of crisp dough that reminded Jaika of potato chips. As she ate, she thought of home, of Mattie and Sam, of her friends in school, and chicken nuggets. She would have loved a chicken nugget.

Davin constantly yelled for his cup to be refilled, and their server would quickly oblige with another bottle of Aurian Red. This young girl could not have been more than twelve years old. She wore her hair in a long braid and a pinafore style apron. Richard kept asking if all of this was a good idea. Davin would only snarl and dismiss his partner saying things about tomorrow being good enough.

Jaika tried to talk with Eli, their server. She learned her name and how the death of her father had led her to a job here in the tavern. Her brother let her sleep at his home, but mostly she worked. Jaika tried to ask her about the king, but Davin threatened to remove her head if she continued to talk.

After the meal, the round lady with the bun led them to rooms upstairs. Davin paid her with coins, then she took them to two rooms. Again the partners argued, but in the end Jaika would have to share a room with Davin. She was given two blankets and a pillow for the floor. Davin laid down on the bed and started making gurgled snores.

Jaika sat on her blankets on the floor for what seemed like hours planning her next move. The house was growing quiet as more and more patrons settled down for the night. If she could just make it out of the inn, there would be plenty of places to hide. But that would not be enough. There was a part of her that wanted more than just escape. She wanted to know the truth about who she was and her life before Mattie, and there was always the people in the mine to consider. She had never met any of them, but they were always with her.

One of her blankets was thin and smooth like the sheets on her bed in Mattie's house. She removed the cover from her pillow and carried the thinnest blanket into the shadows. Standing as far away from the bed as possible, Jaika went to work on the sheet. With her teeth, she tore at the edges, ripping the sheet into long, ragged strips. She then rolled each strip and stuffed it into the empty pillow case.

Davin had at least seven cups of Aurian Red at

dinner. That should knock him out for a while, but she watched his every breath as she worked just to be sure. Each time he stirred, she would melt deeper into the silent shadows until he was still again and it was safe to work. He would not be much of a problem, for now. It was Richard who would cause her the most trouble.

Crawling on her knees, Jaika took four of her torn strips and set to work. Tenderly she wrapped Davin's ankle and secured it to the bed post using three of the strips. She had to be careful not to wrap too tightly or the pain in his ankle might cause him to wake. And that she could not afford.

When both ankles were done, she moved to his hands. He slept flat on his back with his right arm slung above his head. That one was easy to tie to the headboard, but his left rested across his stomach. Watching his face for any indication of life, Jaika lifted his hand. Inch by inch she pulled his hand toward the headboard. It was dead weight in her grip. Three more ties and it too was secure. She knew the ties would not stop him forever, but they would give her extra time to escape, precious time.

Now for Richard.

She could have left him. She could sneak past his door without making a sound, but she wanted his knife. The knife he kept strapped to his belt. The knife she had practiced with. The knife she could balance on one finger and use to hit a target the size of a plate. The knife she would use to kill a king.

Drawing on her hours of training, she moved with shadowy stealth. Jaika opened the door to her room and peered down the empty hallway. Luck was with her – for now. Carrying the pillow case peddler style across her back, she slithered toward Richard's room...the one next to hers.

The knob turned in her hand slowly releasing the latch and opening the door into his room. Jaika could hear Richard's soft, rhythmic breathing as she cracked the door. He had refused the Aurian Red during the meal, so his sleep would not be as heavy as Davin's. She would have to be extra careful.

Leaving the door open just a sliver, Jaika slipped to his side. Richard had removed his shirt and boots, but still wore the black uniform pants of Kaleus's soldiers. In the shadows, Jaika could see the scar across his chest, raised and jagged. Somewhere in the back of her thoughts, she could hear the rushing water and the cracking of the bridge. Who are you, she thought? How could you save my life once and now try to destroy it?

With a trembling hand, Jaika reached toward his chest as if touching the scar might provide some answers. Before her fingers could reach his skin, Richard pounced. Grabbing her wrists, he flipped her onto the floor pinning her to the carpet with his weight.

"What are you up to, Princess?" He smiled with triumph.

Jaika could only stare into his gloating face. Besides the surprise of his attack, she had bumped her head on the floor leaving her dazed and unable to answer.

"Ughhh," she moaned, rolling her head to the side and squinting with the pain.

To Jaika's surprise, Richard sat straight up, releasing her wrists. "Did I hurt you?" He asked looking both worried and remorseful.

Before she could answer, something swished through the air connecting with the side of Richard's head. He collapsed to the floor unconscious. Jaika stared wide-eyed into the face of the tiny servant girl from the dining room.

"I knew they would try to hurt you," she whispered. "I couldn't let them." Her body trembled sending shivers down the board in her hand. She was still fully dressed.

Jaika sat up and rubbed the back of her head. "Thanks," she said, but somehow she didn't think Richard would have hurt her. She turned his head to the side and felt above his ear. He would have a headache in the morning, but the swelling was not bad. He would survive.

So she glanced around the room for her sack of ties lost in the struggle.

Eli pushed it forward with her foot. "Is this what you're looking for?"

"Yes," Jaika said and motioned toward the board still in her friend's hand. "Put that down and help me tie him up."

Together they bound his wrists and feet. Jaika even tied a strip across his mouth. *When he wakes up, he is going to start yelling.*

She found his knife still in the sheath attached to his belt draped across a chair. The belt was too long for her, but an extra loop made it fit her tiny waist quite nicely. As an afterthought, she placed a pillow under his head. She didn't want him to be too uncomfortable.

Eli looked confused but never asked any questions.

"Do you have a safe place to go?" Jaika picked up the board and moved toward the door.

"My brother's house," Eli nodded, staring at the unconscious man on the floor. "When he wakes up, he will come after you."

"By the time he finds me, it won't matter anymore." Jaika wished she didn't have to leave him there. For some odd reason, he had always made her feel safe, at least safer than with Davin or Torin. Even when he had pinned her to the floor she believed he would never really harm her.

In the hallway, Eli motioned for Jaika to follow her. Together, they walked down a back stairway and to an outside door. This door opened directly across from the stables.

Again, luck was on her side. No guard stood at the door, so they entered totally undetected. 1, 2, 3, 4...the fourth stall held Jaika's saktar. He nuzzled her hand in happy greeting.

"You can have Richard's mount." Jaika pointed to a red saktar stabled beside hers.

"No," Eli whispered. "I cannot ride."

"Then I will take you," she nodded. This tiny girl had tried to save her life, so they would ride together to find her brother.

Jaika lifted her saddle from the top railing. Once saddled and ready, Eli rode behind her. She held so tightly to Jaika's stomach that she could hardly breathe, but Jaika did not complain. This girl had risked her life to help her. A little discomfort was a small price to pay.

Together they traveled deeper into the city. She could see the great castle walls as they rode. Shadowy soldiers scattered along the top of the rock walls. Each held a weapon of some type, but the darkness made it impossible to see what it might have been. As unfriendly as the shadowy city felt, Jaika was almost certain she saw a faint sparkle in the walls that the darkness could not hide.

Six smaller towers surrounded one of at least twice their size. Walls and walkways connected the towers, both to the center and along the sides. A yellow-orange light glowed from the many windows in the higher parts of the structure. Jaika could see the smallest tower in the very back of the castle. It should be close to the king's room of prayer. The room she had practiced so long to invade.

Because of the late hour, the city was still and quiet. The soft plodding of Jaika's saktar made an eerie sound in the empty streets. Laughter poured from the windows of one stone building where people appeared to be eating. The inner edge of the city was marked by awning-covered carts and shops, but what Jaika saw of the rest of the city was haunting.

The small houses were crudely built. Some had mud roofs and sagging doors. Even in the poorest neighborhoods of Earth, she had never seen such poverty. The city looked worn and afraid.

Following Eli's confused directions, it took over an hour to reach their destination, but it was worth it to see her safely home. Harin, Eli's brother, offered Jaika his thanks along with a black cloak to keep her warm. His house looked no richer than the others in the city. She felt guilty for accepting the cloak, but it would hide her face from the soldiers and there was still so much to do.

As they waved good-bye, Jaika and Eli knew they would always remember this night.

Secret Door

The king's castle stood tall in the light of the red moon. Jaika had to hurry if she was going to make his morning prayers. Urging her saktar, Jaika weaved her way through the city and around the edges of the castle. Small rock houses and market tents cluttered the roadways. Here and there a light flickered inside a home, and Jaika thought of the children and mothers and fathers who slept and ate in those homes without ever knowing she was here. She missed Mattie, but was glad she was not around to worry. This was surely a time for worry.

When she could clearly see the base of the castle wall, she dismounted. Jaika tied her saktar to a railing outside some sort of restaurant. She could hear laughter and music inside. They would never notice one more saktar.

Pulling the hood of her cloak tight around her

face, Jaika melted into the shadowy darkness. A good hundred yards of clear ground stood between her and the castle walls. Everything was just as the map had shown. Merchants, houses, even the tent of the prophetess.

From this distance, the castle appeared smooth as glass. Each piece of the rock wall interlaced so tightly that it would be impossible to climb. There were no gaps or protruding edges to provide a hand or foot hold. Going up would not be an option, so she decided to stick to the plan.

Staying close to the city's buildings, Jaika worked her way along the edge of the city, slinking from shadow to shadow, building to building, until she could see the archway. Just as Davin had said, a slim rock archway obscured by a low growing vine. Even without the vine, the shape of the door was made almost invisible by the patterns in the rocks. The architect of such an entrance was truly a master of disguise. And again, just as Oberon's informant had predicted, there was no guard, save one atop the wall. Jaika shuttered to think who this informant might be and just how close he was to Merith. Who could have told Oberon about the guards and especially the secret room?

Jaika shivered inside her cloak despite the sticky air. Trying to still the loud thumping of her heart, she watched the guard scanning the city for intruders. He had not seen her — yet.

Jaika

The minutes ticked by with Jaika pressed against the wall of an empty shop straining to remain perfectly still, waiting for her chance. The muscles in her calves ached. After what seemed like hours, it happened — the guard turned his back to the city. Jaika sprinted the one hundred yards to the archway. Throwing her full weight against the door, it swung inward, and Jaika fell through. She collapsed onto the dirt floor drinking in the stale air and trying hard to remain calm. A narrow hallway leading into a wall of darkness was all she could see. Jaika stood up, threw her back against the door, and pushed it shut. The metal bolt slid into place, and then she was alone.

She had practiced moving in the dark inside Kaleus's fortress, but it was nothing like this. A blindfold could never have prepared her for the caged-animal terror that ran through her skin. Her mind imagined all kinds of small, hairy creatures hiding in the velvety blackness. She strained to hear the guards outside and anything that might be inside...with her. She took a deep breath and focused on slowing her heart.

Jaika raised her hand to her face, but her eyes saw nothing, not even an outline or a shadow. She was blanketed in the darkness. Her breath quivered, echoing along the walls of the corridor. It was the only sound within the long hallway. Jaika fought the fear that raced through her legs and gripped her stomach. She wanted to run and never come back. She thought of Seela's son and the people in the mine. So many people depending on her. *The door was on the left, Davin had said. The door to the prayer room was on the left.*

Jaika ran her hands across the door and over to the left wall. Keeping her back to that wall, she began to edge forward shushing the dirt floor beneath her feet. *1, 2, 3...* she counted her steps in her mind. *4, 5, 6...*

The hallway walls were of the same rough cut rock as the outside of the castle. The silky-smooth appearance from the outside had been only an illusion. The edges of the rock caught on Jaika's cloak, snagging and pulling, sometimes digging into her hands. Her hood was soon pulled back to her shoulders, but Jaika did not take her hands away from the wall to right it. She just kept moving... *21, 22...*

She fought the urge to yell out, 'Is anybody there?' — a reply would have been much worse than the silence. Instead, she inched forward for what felt like miles of hallway stopping only to listen for footsteps. *55, 56...*

Then the wall grew smooth. Jaika stopped, listening again, hearing only her ragged breath and the pounding of her heart. Sliding her hands forward, she felt along this new doorway. She could feel the tiny creases between each plank of wood and eventually a handle. Her fingers quickly wrapped around it and pulled, bringing her one step closer to her destination.

She turned the handle, and the door opened with a loud squeal. Jaika froze, waiting for the soldiers to burst into the hallway, dragging her away — but no one came. She slid her feet across the ground and through the doorway. Afraid that if she lifted them to take a genuine step, she would never again find the floor.

She tried to envision the room... the altar protruding out of the front wall where the lights should be, the dozen or so chairs in the middle of the room, the warrior statues that stood in the two front corners. All of this was somewhere in this black fog.

Jaika closed the door and slumped against it. *What time is it? How long is this taking? Are Davin and Richard still tied up?* The questions raced through her mind, but Jaika shook them away. *Find the statue. That comes first. Find the statue.*

She could not afford to travel along the altar wall. The altar held candles and pottery bowls. Anything she knocked over would alert the king to her presence. She would have to walk through the center of the room.

Jaika took one step forward on the stone floor...now two. Without the wall for support, her senses swam. Front, back, up, down, her body floated in the sea of darkness. She panicked and collapsed to the floor with a whimper. Stretching out with her hands, her fingers found the door, and she slid back across the cold stone to cower against it. *Now what?*

Jaika clung to the door until her breathing slowed to a more controllable level. Again she tried to imagine the room. Davin had described nothing along the back wall. *Was it empty? How long? Was his information even right?* She would have to chance it.

Leaning against the door, Jaika forced herself to stand. Again, with her back to the wall, feeling along the rocks, she edged forward. In no time, she reached the corner of the room and turned to slide along the back wall. The room was shallow, so the side walls were short.

Her fingers danced across the wall, and Jaika moved with less caution. Her arms swung upward catching her fingers on cold metal. It took a moment for Jaika to sense the slice across her palm. She could feel the warm blood dripping from her fingers and the burn when she opened her hand wide. Grimacing with the pain, she wrapped the hem of her cloak around her hand, squeezing it tight, trying to stop the blood. She scolded herself for being so careless. Now she had only one useful hand.

With timid movements, Jaika felt for her attacker. Cold metal, it was only a sword decorating the wall. She moved across it and forward. Slower now, feeling with one hand and holding the other against her. The throbbing pain increased.

Jaika maneuvered the second corner and side wall to reach the warrior stature just where Davin had described. She could feel the smooth stone arm and dimpled chest plate. Her hands could not reach the face, but she knew it was not smiling.

The statue stood well away from the wall, leaving plenty of room for Jaika to nestle back into the corner. Pulling her hood over her face, she melted against the wall to wait. The bleeding had stopped, but the sharp pain crawled down her fingers and up into her wrist. She pulled it close to her chest, leaned her head against the wall, and listened.

Mercy

The slamming door jolted Jaika back to consciousness. Her body fixed rigid and ready to fight. She scanned the darkness until she finally remembered where she was. The prayer room, the castle, she was waiting for *him*. It was not the prayer room door that had awakened her. Another — somewhere along the hallway maybe, or the outer door she had used to enter the castle.

I must have fallen asleep, she thought, blinking and squinting to see through the darkness. When she moved, a sharp pain shot through her hand and arm, and she remembered the sword slicing her palm. Before she could twist to rearrange her position, the metallic click of the door latch stopped her heart. The door to the prayer room scraped slowly against the stone floor. The altar blocked her view, but a torchlight danced around its edges and the sound of at least two pairs of feet entered the room.

"I will wait in the hallway, Sire," a man's voice rumbled against the walls. A voice that echoed with familiarity though Jaika was sure she had never been here before.

The king must have nodded because she heard no reply. The door closed, but the torchlight did not move. She could smell the candles being lit and see the flickering of new light growing and playing across the rock walls of the prayer room. The main light at the front of the room was not made of fire. It looked like the lanterns in Earth's history books, but it held a simple stone pulsing with yellow and white light.

She could just see the outline of Merith's back. He was kneeling now, mumbling, whispering his prayers — unaware that anyone was close. *No sound*, Jaika commanded her feet with her thoughts, *just as I practiced*.

Jaika slid her body up the wall to a standing position, her right hand burning with every movement. Her soft boots had no heavy sole to clump against the ground, but she must still be cautious. There must be no sound.

Wincing from the pain in her hand, she crept from the shadows, holding her breath, waiting to be discovered. She pulled her hood up over her face in an effort to hide even deeper in the shadows.

Merith never wavered from his prayers.

Walking only on tiptoe, Jaika moved toward his

back. No breath, not even her cloak was allowed to rustle against the stone floor. Her body moved with the very shadows.

Behind him now, his shoulders were not as broad as she'd imagined. No crown, no shining clothes like Kaleus wore. A tiny, prickling doubt nagged at the back of her thoughts. *What if he isn't the king? What if this is the wrong man?*

Forcing herself to concentrate on the moment, she unsheathed the knife that dangled from her belt — Richard's knife. Still no sound. One more step and she could touch him. Another step and the knife slipped silently to his throat.

She heard the catch in his breath, saw his shoulders tighten, but he never faltered.

"Listen and I will spare your life." Her words were hushed, raspy. The guard must not hear.

Merith made no response.

Jaika pulled the knife a whisper away from his neck afraid the trembling in her hand would cause an unintentional wound.

"I was sent by Kaleus to kill you. Two others will also come. You have a spy. Someone you trust sends information to Kaleus by Talec bird. He knows your schedule, your guard changes, the castle layout ... everything."

She could see the king's back relax — just a bit.

"I will give you what information I have, but I need something in return." Jaika stepped back still holding the knife.

Merith dropped his head in relief. "What do you want from me?" His voice did not sound the least bit afraid.

Jaika swallowed hard. "When I am punished for attacking the king, I want to be executed." She drew a ragged breath. "In public," she whispered. "Everyone must see so that Kaleus will know I have failed."

Merith stood slowly, blocking the alter light. Only a hand or two taller than Jaika, but at this moment, Jaika was sure he was twice her height.

She took another step backward. She couldn't stop the quivering sound of her breath or the trembling in her hands.

Merith turned to face her. Dark clothes, simple black tunic. His face was in shadow, but she could still see his anger. His eyes glared at the cloaked figure before him.

"Show me your face!" He commanded, pronouncing each word with deliberate force.

Jaika took another step back. *What if he kills me here? No one will know. All those people will die. Why isn't he afraid?*

"Pleeease," she whispered, the words of a pleading, scolded child.

Merith eyes flashed with confusion. "Show me your face!" Again his strong words.

Jaika dropped the knife with a dull thud.

Merith never turned his eyes away.

With timid movements, Jaika pulled her hood down to her shoulders, her dark, coarse hair cascaded around her face. Her dark eyes shone with both fear and defiance.

Merith gasped — never moving, his eyes devouring her face, searching her eyes, as if trying to see into her very soul.

When he did move, it was quick and without warning. Jaika raised her arms to defend against his attack, but no blow was struck. Instead he encircled her with his arms and crushed her against his body. "My Jaika," his only words.

Over and over he whispered her name until she melted against his strength. Collapsing into his arms, the fear spilling from her body in the form of silent tears. This was the first person who had held her since Mattie's death. The first kindness she had tasted in so long. Jaika had lived only in fear, and it all came rushing to the surface. She released everything to this man.

She wasn't sure who this man was, but he certainly knew her. And what's more, he cared for her. His voice, his embrace, there was no mistake. He knew and loved her.

Sobs wracked her body, as he stroked her hair, rocking gently as a mother might rock her infant child. She wanted to stay here forever, with this kind man who so obviously loved her.

When she finally quieted, he pulled her away to study her face. He wiped the tears from her eyes with his fingertips, and for the first time, she could see his face clearly. He was not a tall man, but there was a definite power emanating from within. Strong, square face, worn with time and struggle, but his eyes held such joy.

"I want to hear everything." He whispered the words, but they were a command just the same. "But for now you must trust me." He pulled Jaika's hood over her face stretching it low to cover her eyes and hide any stray curls.

She did not resist. The last of her strength was spent.

"Captain!" He shouted.

Immediately the door opened. A broad, mountain of a man entered the prayer room. The gray streaks in his hair and beard were the only indication of his advanced age. He wore black pants tucked into knee high boots and a gray soldier's tunic.

When he saw the cloaked figure beside the king, he drew his sword. "Merith!" He warned, tensing for battle, waiting only for the king's command to strike.

"I am safe, my friend." Merith motioned to put

away the sword. "But I do need your help."

The soldier sheathed his sword without question and nodded.

"This...man...is to be taken to my chambers. Provide him with food and drink, but only by your hand. No one else is to know of his existence." This soldier dwarfed the king, but Merith's power was inescapable. "Use the tunnel."

The soldier raised his eyebrow in question. "I understand."

Jaika didn't think he understood at all, but she would try to trust this man just the same.

Merith turned to Jaika. "He is Keshar, the Captain of my army. You can trust him to protect you." He lifted his hand as if he would touch her face and then thought better of it.

"Follow me, sir." Keshar ordered.

Jaika smiled beneath the hood when he called her sir.

Keshar grabbed a torch that hung from a metal rack in the hallway and led her into the darkness — away from the hidden archway door and deeper into the castle. Shadows danced along the rocks as they walked, and an oily smoke trail floated behind the torch. He threw Jaika a concerned glance every now and again, his face full of questions, but he never spoke.

Jaika

The hallway ended abruptly with a series of short steps leading down into yet another rock hallway. This one was narrow and stank of dust and mildew. The heavy air stirred around them as though unused to travelers. Jaika tightened her cloak to block the chill.

Keshar was aware of her movements but still said nothing. Jaika was glad he didn't ask any questions. It would be hard to explain that she had come here to kill the man he worked for.

The rock hallway twisted and turned until Jaika lost all sense of direction. It ended in a wall of stairs, steep stairs, almost straight up with a thin door at the top. Keshar ascended the stairs with ease, his torch steady.

Jaika heard a key turn and the door swung open. Still another key turn, and light burst forward onto the stairway. Keshar doused his torch then slipped it into a metal ring beside the door. Pulling back what looked like a long curtain, he motioned for Jaika to follow.

I am glad Keshar had to carry the torch, she thought as she maneuvered the slippery stairs and the narrow doorway. The entrance led her into a large bedroom. This room was at least four times the size of her bedroom in Mattie's house. The three side windows were bare. The four-poster bed on the far wall had a rough, wooly curtain tied back at each post. The bed was covered in worn blankets with several pillows. A table hid in one corner, a writing desk by the left wall. Surely not the room of a king. Maybe she had tried to kill the wrong man after all.

Looking back, Jaika could see that they had not come through a curtain at all. It had, instead, been a cape. A cape hanging inside a wooden cabinet. A wardrobe used for storage. Jaika thought of the stories Mattie had read to her as a child and wished this wardrobe led somewhere other than a cold, lifeless tunnel.

"I will return after I have escorted King Merith." Keshar offered a curt bow and climbed back into the cabinet closing the door behind him.

Jaika heard the key turn in the lock, and then again in the tunnel door.

"Just great," Jaika sighed pulling off her dirt stained cloak.

Tossing it on the desk chair, Jaika wandered about the room. She ran her fingers along the fabrics that surrounded the bed and picked up a book that she couldn't read. On the far side of the bed, she found a sliver of a table holding a bowl of fruit and some sort of drink in a tall glass bottle.

"I did miss breakfast," she smirked, kicking off her boots.

Jaika flopped onto the bed bouncing pillows in all directions. She slid her hand across the blankets. It had been a long time since she'd slept in a real bed — a very long time. She settled her head against the pillows and snuggled deep into the blankets. She decided breakfast could wait.

A Plan

Jaika slept for most of the day. The shadows were long when the bedroom door opened. Merith and Keshar entered the room followed by a cloaked stranger. He walked slowly as with fatigue. The princess rubbed her eyes and yawned, trying to shake the sleep away as she strained to see in the dim light and to remember where she was.

Merith slid back two panels in the wall to reveal a row of glowers growing in a long, narrow window box anchored to the inside wall. Yellow light quickly poured into every dark corner.

"A woman?" Keshar looked wide eyed from Jaika to Merith and back again.

The cloaked figure slid the hood from his face to reveal an annoyingly happy smile. "That's Jaika," he announced.

"No!" Jaika screamed. Fighting her way out of the pillows, she dove for the cloaked man.

But, Keshar was faster than the scrambling princess. With little effort, he scooped her into his arms before she could reach her target.

Held by the waist, Jaika flailed her arms and kicked helplessly at the air. "He was sent to kill the king!" she shrieked. "He's one of Kaleus's men!"

Keshar erupted in laughter, a deep belly laugh that shook his whole body and loosened his grip.

Jaika slipped from his grasp and crumbled to the floor in frustration. "Will someone please tell me what is going on?" Obviously, no one else was afraid of Richard.

"This man is my son." Keshar's words intermingled with his laughter. "And he certainly will not kill Merith."

Richard shifted uneasily under his cloak. "I'm sorry I had to deceive you." The sincere concern in his gentle eyes made it impossible for Jaika to be angry any longer.

"I still don't understand," Jaika repeated softly, shaking her head and looking from Richard to Keshar for answers.

"We knew Kaleus had reconstructed the SolStone to find you." Merith spoke for the first time since he had entered his chamber. "I sent Richard to protect you in case he succeeded."

"It was an honor to protect his daughter." Richard lowered his head in a partial bow.

Jaika caught her breath and turned her eyes to Merith. "Daughter?" she questioned.

Merith smiled, and for a moment he looked just like the young king in Jaika's dreams. "You didn't know?" He whispered.

"I never got a chance to tell her," Richard shrugged.

"You're my father?" Jaika could not believe the words. She stared into his face trying to understand. So much had happened in the last few days — the journey across the sands, the Breen's attack, and her escape. Now Richard was here, and he was not working for Kaleus. He did not want to kill this man. So where was Davin? Who was he loyal to? It was becoming difficult to even think at all.

"My father is a king," she whispered. "All this time I thought..." Jaika's words trembled, and she looked away.

In one step, Merith was near his daughter, lifting her from the floor and pulling her close. "I sent you away to protect you." He whispered close to her ear. "Not one day has passed that I did not think of you. That I did not miss you desperately."

Jaika studied his adoring face. "My father really is a king." Her words still sounded unconvinced.

Merith laughed and hugged her close.

Somehow she must have known last night in the prayer room. It had been so perfect when he held her, and it was perfect now. This was truly where she belonged.

"My lord..." Keshar cleared his throat. "There is not much time."

"Of course," releasing Jaika, Merith resumed his formal countenance.

Jaika wiped at the corner of her eye.

"Richard has already provided us with a great deal of information concerning Kaleus's fortress." Merith nodded. "It appears impenetrable."

"Who is the mole?" Jaika asked.

"What in Alapi is a mole?" Keshar asked.

"A spy. You know, the person giving Kaleus your secrets."

Richard flipped the side of his cloak over his shoulder revealing a gray tunic. The same gray tunic of Merith's soldiers. "The informant is new. Kaleus has only been receiving his messages for the past few moons. A Talec bird brings the information."

Keshar sneered, running his fingers through his tousled, graying hair. "A Talec bird, ehhh. That should be easy enough to find."

"If we stop this spy, we could send false information." Richard planned, pacing around the room.

"That could give us a tactical advantage," Keshar agreed.

"Advantage or not, his forces still outnumber ours three to one." Merith moved to the window to study the city beyond, grasping for a solution to Kaleus.

Jaika sat down on the edge of the bed. She thought of Levek and his kindness, of Seela's delicate face, of Torin and the children he will never have. She did not want to fight any of them. Why must war be the only answer? "Poor Torin," she whispered, not realizing she had spoken her thoughts out loud.

"Poor Torin?" Richard crossed to stand at her side. "What do you mean 'poor Torin?' Torin was cruel to you." He took her hand in his as he spoke.

Jaika shook her head. "He was always so sad."

"How can you worry about such a man?"

"He did not deserve to lose his wife..." Jaika stopped. Her eyes burned through Richard as though he were not there. She gripped his hand hard until he jerked it away.

"Jaika?" he breathed, throwing her a crushed look.

"I'm sorry...I just...Richard, tell me about the crystal mines."

Confusion clouded his eyes. "What about the

mines?"

"Where are they?" Jaika rushed. "How many guards? What's inside?"

Richard stood, staring down at Jaika, backing away, almost frightened. He knew exactly what she was planning. "And carry destruction to the lesser king." He mumbled the words like a familiar children's song. He had joined with Kaleus to protect his friend... his love, but, he had never really believed she would fulfill the prophecy. He never believed she would help to defeat Kaleus.

Richard turned and grabbed his father's arm. "It will work. She's right. The mines. It would only take a few men. Everything would change." His words gushed, nonsensical.

Keshar gripped his shoulders and shook him hard. "What are you talking about, boy?"

Richard took a deep breath and started over. "We don't need to defeat Kaleus's army."

Merith raise his eyebrows with interest. "Go on," he insisted.

"Many in his army obey to save those in the mines. If we free the mine workers, his army will collapse."

"He's right," Jaika interjected. "Torin, my guard, only stayed with me to protect his wife, Mara. She's a prisoner in the mines. Kaleus said he would kill her if I escaped. That's why I wanted a public execution."

"You asked for an execution?" Richard gasped.

"I had to be sure Kaleus knew I failed. It was the only way I could make sure no one else would die."

Richard shook his head in disbelief. "You would have died for people in the mines? People you don't even know?"

"She *is* my daughter." Merith boasted.

"So, Richard, tell us about the mines." Keshar prompted.

Jaika watched as all three men assumed an air of battle. Merith pulled a small table from the wall and each man grabbed various chairs from around the room.

Using the table decorations as markers, Richard laid out a map and a plan of attack. "The mines are in the Great Mountains. Two guards stand here. Ten more work inside here..."

Jaika curled up on the bed, letting their words of war float past. She would look for Mara first. Torin would be surprised...

As they planned, Merith watched his daughter from the corner of his eye. Seeing her settle in among the pillows, her breathing became rhythmic and he knew she was sleeping again. For the first time since he could remember, he felt like there was truly hope for his people. Maybe his Jaika really was the one to bring peace back to Regar.

Jaika

As they completed the plan, Merith realized that there was another in the castle who should know about the attack, should know about Jaika. He turned to Richard and firmly gripped his shoulder. "Thank you for protecting my daughter. Working under Kaleus was dangerous, and I am grateful." He looked over his shoulder at Jaika. "Let her sleep for now. I will send someone to relieve you so that you can prepare, but there is something I must do first."

Richard nodded, "I will stay with her."

He left her sleeping under Richard's care and headed off down the hallway with Keshar close behind. There was always a guard assigned to Merith, but most of his soldiers were protecting Palon. So, this was Keshar's duty for now. He knew where his king was going. He knew the man he needed to see — the only person in the castle who loved Jaika as much as her father.

They climbed the narrow stairs to the south tower where the Guardians worked. The hallways here became narrower with stairs that spiraled and climbed to the highest towers in the castle. The rooms were tiny and oddly shaped with only basic furnishings. A bed, a chair, and maybe a table. The simplistic rooms of the Guardians.

Galimar responded to the first knock. "Yes, my lord," he was surprised to see Merith.

Merith smiled, and Galimar knew something wonderful must have happened. It had been many years since his king had looked this hopeful, this determined... this young. "Please, come inside. Eron and I were working."

"She's here," Merith proclaimed, walking into the tiny room. He gave Eron a respectful nod. These two men were seldom apart, so it was no surprise to find them working side-by-side. "She has come back to us. The information we received was accurate. Jaika is here."

"Your daughter?" Eron mumbled.

Galimar shook his head. He had given up long ago. Injuries and age had taken most of his agility as well as his hope. "How can you be sure?"

"You need to see her," he said. "You'll know when you see her."

Galimar looked to Keshar for confirmation, but he seemed ready to accept whatever Merith believed without question.

"She has the birthmark," Merith spoke undaunted. "She recognized Richard from his scar. She remembered the scar."

"She remembers the accident at the bridge?" Galimar questioned. Many knew that story. It would not be hard for someone to feign a memory.

"Yes, Richard was the one who saved her from drowning." Eron's eyes sparkled with understanding.

"Richard said she was not told. There was no one

at Kaleus's castle who would know the story. Besides, they would have killed Richard long ago if they had known the truth." Merith paused, imploring his friend to accept his story. He had watched his daughter's loss quietly destroy this man, but it could be different now. "She remembered. She has to be our Jaika."

Galimar gripped the edge of his wooden desk to lower himself into his chair. He looked toward Eron wondering just how much of the past he held on to. "Does she remember me?"

Merith hesitated. "I do not know. We have only spoken of Kaleus and what she experienced there."

Galimar winced, "If she remembers the bridge, then she must also remember..."

"You," Merith interrupted. "Your goodness, your strength, that is what she remembers."

Galimar knew the king was being kind. He did not blame him for his failures. It was Galimar who could not forgive himself. "Then I must speak with her."

"Yes. We have a plan... to free the workers in the mines. Jaika believes the soldiers will desert once their families are safe. Kaleus uses the workers in the mine as leverage to force those around him to obey. If he loses that leverage, we could win the day. We don't have to defeat the army — just stop them from fighting. Think of the lives we could save."

"Are you taking Jaika with you?"

The king paused. Merith looked at his friend, remembering all that he had done for him and his daughter, his work with the SolStone, his sacrifice as a soldier. "I do not want to take her with me. I want to leave her with you. Will you stay behind? Will you protect her? If we fail at the mines, you know Kaleus's army will come. Whether he leads them or Oberon, it matters not, they will come." Merith closed his eyes imagining the destruction of his world if he failed. "I will take a handful of my strongest men, but I need you here."

"You have only to ask."

"I also," Eron agreed. "We will do what needs to be done."

These men had never failed him, and for this he was grateful. He knew they would keep Jaika safe.

#

As the sleep cleared from Jaika's eyes, it was hard to remember where she was. Her muscles were heavy with sleep – the peaceful, deep, hypnotic sleep that her days spent in a prison cell had made impossible. She thought about Mattie and Oberon and Seela and Torin and all the things she had seen since she arrived on Regar. And now she was in her father's house. She was in a castle with a man she could hardly remember and trying to stop a war she knew very little about. She still had so many questions and that made it even harder to listen to Richard when he returned with the others.

"What do you mean stay here?" Jaika raged red faced. She bolted to her feet beside her father's bed glaring in defiance. "I will not stay here!" Suddenly Jaika wasn't sure if she could really trust these people. Or if she could trust her memories. What if her father was not going to save the workers? What if he had a different plan altogether? What if Richard really did work for Oberon or Kaleus and was planning something horrible after they left the castle. She wasn't really sure who was on her side anymore.

Behind Merith, in the shadow of the doorway, Galimar spoke from beneath his cloak. "I am Galimar," his voice heavy and wise. "I will stay with you. I will protect you, Jaika. I will not let anyone hurt you. Eron will be here as well. You will be safe."

"Galimar?" Jaika puzzled.

Richard fumbled with the shoulder strap that held his sword, wishing away her anger. "Please, Jaika," he cautioned. "The mines will be dangerous. The guards will not leave without a fight, and Kaleus does have his truly loyal followers, those who don't care about the people in the mines."

Richard watched as Jaika threw up her hands in frustration, huffing and pacing the king's chambers. Kaleus's men would kill her without hesitation and that was something Richard would never allow. Something none of them would allow.

"Why won't you let me come? Has there been a change in the plan?"

Richard's face grew warm at the power of his feelings for her. "What if we can't protect you?" Richard protested, lowering his eyes. "We don't want to lose you again."

Jaika flinched. His words were soft, and she knew they were difficult to say. She had not expected his tender reaction, and her pulse quickened.

"You protected me as a child, didn't you?" Jaika studied his expression, unsure of her question. There was still so much from her childhood she didn't remember. "You protected me. That's how you got that scar on your chest?"

Richard met her gaze full on knowing he would suffer a thousand scars to keep her safe. "That's when I knew I'd truly found you — that day in the training room, when you saw the scar, when you called me Ree. Only the real Jaika would know that scar — that name."

Jaika remembered the rushing water. She tingled with the memories of her childhood nightmares and the shadowy faces. She knew it wasn't the wisest decision, but she wanted to go with Richard, with the soldiers. She wanted to free the people in the mines and maybe even find Mara.

"Let me ride with you." Jaika tried again, waiting

for his argument. "I will follow your orders. Whatever you tell me I will do, but please don't leave me here." Her firm stance could not disguise the pleading in her voice.

She was safer with him than anywhere else, Richard reasoned. Even in Merith's castle not everyone could be trusted and at least one of Kaleus's spies still roamed free. Besides, it would be nice to have her with him, even for a short time.

A mischievous smile played across his face as he relented. "Anything I say?" Richard mocked, forgetting the others watched.

Jaika knew he was no longer talking about the upcoming battle and that he'd changed his mind about leaving her behind.

"Anything at all," she whispered, never taking her eyes from his. She held her breath for a moment hoping he would touch her face or maybe even kiss her, but instead he turned away.

"You will stay here," he said, tossing the careless words over his shoulder as he left the room. In his heart, he knew if he stayed in the room, he would be powerless to leave her behind.

Merith couldn't help but feel pleased knowing that when age or war took his life and that of his most trusted allies, Richard would still be there for Jaika.

That evening as the sun set, Keshar led ten of Merith's finest soldiers beneath the shadow of the Great

Mountain Range and Regar's two moons. Shrouded in black cloaks, ten mounted soldiers followed their captain and their king across the waterless sands toward Kaleus's crystal mines. Jaika watched helplessly as their silhouettes faded into the darkness. Even the power of the red moon was not strong enough to hold them back.

Galimar

Not sure where else to go, Jaika hid in Merith's chambers. Galimar and Eron waited with her in an uncomfortable silence. She wanted desperately to remember them, but her past felt so far away.

Eron stood and stretched, rolling his neck from side to side. His hood draping around his shoulders. "I'm not a very good guard, am I?" he smiled rubbing his eyes. "I am having trouble staying awake."

Jaika nodded, amused at her protector. "Well, I am safe, so everything is fine."

Eron nodded.

"Do you remember me?" Jaika questioned, taking a chance that one of these men would share more information than Richard or her father.

"I remember you as a little girl, bouncing and running around – always running around." Eron settled back in his chair looking tired. His once youthful naivety stolen away by years of war. "I looked different then. I *was* different then." He stared at Jaika. "*Everything* was different then."

She studied the red scar beneath his eye and wondered what might have happened. "So you were here when I was young?"

"I have been a Guardian for as long as I can remember," Eron mused with a faraway look in his eyes. "I worked with Galimar in the temple. I was there when he sent you away with the SolStone." He closed his eyes, remembering the blue light.

Jaika stiffened, looking to the hooded figure by the door. "Galimar, you are the one who sent me to Earth?" she questioned, unsure of this man who would not remove his cloak. "I only remember pieces. I remember a lady and my necklace. My necklace that Oberon took. She wore it, but then they gave it to me when she died..." Jaika sighed, "I can't even see her face."

Galimar tilted his head so she knew he was listening.

"Were we here, in this castle, when you sent me through the doorway, when you used the SolStone?"

Galimar moved closer to the door making sure his face was turned away. "No, we were in the Guardian's temple at the edge of the desert along the Great Mountains where no one could find us. That is where I used the SolStone."

Jaika nodded. "Seela told me about the SolStone."

"What's a Seela?" Eron said.

"She is a Tal woman who works for Kaleus. Her son is in the mines. She taught me to speak Regarian – in the castle with Oberon. He has the SolStone now. He used it to come and get me. How did he do that?"

Galimar hesitated, not sure how to answer. He knew he had lied when she was a child... when he sent her away with the stone. He had no idea how to find her once she was through the light. He knew the route. He knew where they would be, but he did not know how long they would stay there. If she moved very far from that brick building, he would never have found her. He did know Inita's pendant was important since it had once been part of the SolStone but not how to use it. "I know it had something to do with the pendant. It was broken from the SolStone."

Eron giggled. "And then it was broken into a million pieces. Right, Galimar?"

His friend did not answer.

"After he sent you through, Galimar smashed it into a thousand pieces. Then they blew up the temple. Pieces went everywhere." He raised his hand to touch the scar under his eye. "Everywhere."

"So if you broke it into pieces, how were you going to find me?"

Galimar's chest rose in a heavy sigh. "I wasn't."

Jaika's heart quivered.

"With the SolStone destroyed we could not find you, but then...neither could Kaleus. If he defeated our soldiers the SolStone would belong to him, and he would find you."

"But he does have the SolStone, at least Oberon does. How did he get it?"

"Oberon pieced it back together. He came back to the ruins of the temple to find the shards. He does not have the entire stone, but he has enough."

Jaika now understood why Oberon's pendant had looked jagged and incomplete.

"He used a lot of people," Eron added. "A lot of people to dig for those pieces. That was the beginning... he used the workers for everything... everyone was afraid of the stone."

He stood and rubbed his eyes. "Forgive me, but I need to go for a walk. I need something to clear my mind, or I will be of no use to you."

Galimar nodded, his face still cloaked. "Of course my friend. Do what you must." Eron was a grown man, but it was difficult for Galimar to see him as anything but the hope-filled, wide-eyed youth who had worked by his side for more moons that he could count.

As Eron was leaving, Jaika felt her chest tighten at

the thought of being alone with Galimar. She was embarrassed that she couldn't remember him. She didn't know if he was a good man or a bad man. He had sent her through the wall of light, but her father had ordered it. So, was he being brave or being cruel?

Galimar must have been able to feel her apprehension. He turned and apologized for the hood. "Forgive me for keeping my face covered. I am disfigured, and I do not want to make you uncomfortable."

"Disfigured?"

"From battle."

"I thought you were a Guardian. Isn't that like a wise man or a priest?"

"Yes, a Guardian studies the teachings of the creator, Gelquin. But before I was a Guardian, I was a soldier. For many turns I was a soldier. I protected you and your mother." He watched Jaika's face for any sign of memories.

"You knew my mother?"

"Yes, Jaika, for many turns."

"What was she like?"

Galimar could feel her body relax as their conversation shifted. "She was very special – your father loved her deeply. He would have done anything to protect her."

"She died before I left... before you sent me away?"

Her words stung. "Yes, she died when you were young." He could see her trying to find the missing pieces. He knew that her memories had not returned and in his heart he hoped they never would.

"Were you...?" Jaika's words were broken by a knock on the door.

Galimar unlocked the heavy door to reveal a lone soldier. "Forgive me for interrupting, my lord, but you asked us to watch for anything unusual... there is something you must see."

The Guardian nodded to Jaika. If there was danger, then they would face it together.

Talec

Along the narrow walkways of the inner castle they followed the soldier, down several flights of stairs. They eventually emerged in the dim hallway leading to the king's private prayer room. The same hallway Jaika had traveled in complete darkness to kill her father. Two soldiers stood outside the open prayer room. Galimar could see the altar candles flickering as they passed through.

A decorative shield had been removed from the back wall of the prayer room, and a sliver of a door stood open in its place. Galimar had to turn sideways to fit his broad shoulders through the doorway and into the next room.

The tiny room beyond stood empty except for three cages and a footprint covered dirt floor. No windows, and Galimar's tall frame covered the only door. Each cage stood no more than knee high and held the leather hood and straps of a Talec bird.

"The room was empty when we entered, sir." One of the gray tuniced guards announced. The Guardian could hear the regret in his voice.

"How did you find this place?" Galimar questioned, studying the shape of the shoe prints in the dirt. The prints piled upon each other making it difficult to find a clear outline.

"I heard a bird, sir." The young messenger quickly spoke up. "I came to replace the candles. I know I am not allowed to speak of this room, but these soldiers already knew, and I needed help to open the door." His words rattled in nervous explanation.

"Do not be afraid," Galimar assured. "You did the right thing."

Still Galimar stared at the empty cages looking for unseen answers. How long had this been here without detection. And why had the bird called out? It was unusual for a trained Talec to make a sound. A sharp knife could make sure of that. So something... no... someone must have disturbed it... someone in a hurry.

"How much time has passed since you heard the bird."

"Not long, sir."

"Then the spy may not yet have released the Talec." Galimar spun on his heel sending his cloak flying around him. "Have the upper walls searched. High places...any place a Talec might be released."

"Yes, sir." The guards reported, then sprinted from the prayer room.

Galimar, however, did not follow the soldiers. He chose to leave the castle through the hidden door in the back castle wall. The same arched stone door by which Jaika had invaded Merith's prayers. He pulled Jaika close to his side as he walked.

If the spy knew of the secret passages, he must be someone high in rank, or at least someone who has served a long time in this castle. He might already know they searched for him and the Talec. And worst of all, he would know about Jaika.

Pulling his cloak close to his body, Galimar emerged onto the dusty road along the back wall of Merith's castle. Only the taverns would be selling anything at this time of night, so there would be no one to hinder his search, and no one to see Jaika.

He tried to imagine how Jaika must have felt the night she attacked Merith. She would have emerged from the desert alone and unsure in a strange new city. How much of Regar did she truly remember?

He moved in between the shops and market tents, taking each step with caution, walking blind, never allowing his eyes to leave the top of the castle walls. "Listen and watch Jaika. We must find him before the Talec is lost."

Jaika followed in his steps, watching as Galimar's limp began to disappear and his instincts rush in.

There...a shadow...spirited across the wall. Two more followed. Soldiers...only soldiers. No Talec bird in sight.

One more step. A tent stake, unseen in the darkness, grabbed at Galimar's boot pulling him backward to the ground. In mumbled hisses, he cursed his clumsiness knowing he wasted precious time. But as he stood and dusted his legs, he saw it...the north tower.

The window light was dim, but there was no mistaking it. There was a light within the tower room. Merith... Keshar...they were all gone. The Guardians...who else would need the tower?

"Come!" he commanded as he ran. Stumbling with his first steps, until years of battle-ready training quickly overpowered his hesitation and steadied his feet. He moved as a seasoned warrior, feet flying, carrying him back through the arched stone doorway, down the corridor, through a side door and up a dusty staircase. Jaika followed him upward to the vast endless stairways that would carry him to the north tower. He could hear her behind him. Her steps were quicker and more sure than his own.

Somewhere along the way his Guardian's cloak was cast off to reveal the gray tunic of Merith's army. The tunic he could never bring himself to put away. He must do the work of a soldier now. His stomach sickened at what he knew lay ahead. There was only one person who had access to the tower. One person who did not ride with Merith.

Galimar's muscles ached as he reached the base of the tower stairs. Spiraling stairs, leading only to the top. There were no doors, and no windows between him and the tower room, only stairs.

Two steps at a time he climbed, dreading what lay at the top. He whispered a prayer that he would not be too late.

"Cawree!" The cry of the Talec bird echoed down the stairwell, driving Galimar forward.

By the time he could see the top, his breath was coming in great heaves. Galimar gulped his air and slammed every ounce of his strength against the tower door. Splinters sprayed, the wood around the bolt split, and the door burst sideways.

Before the man at the window even turned, Galimar knew his face. He had not even bothered to remove his robe — his Guardian's robe.

"He will know!" Eron shouted as he gripped the struggling Talec bird. "Oberon will know they are coming!" Eron flung his words as a madman. Teetering on the edge of the window, caught between worlds, he turned to face his friend.

"Why?" Galimar whispered the word, shuttering, trying to catch his breath. His fear settled in his stomach and legs.

"Eron?" Jaika whispered, afraid to move past the doorway.

"Don't you understand?" Eron smiled, his eyes not seeing. The scar beneath his eye burned fiery red. "He did this. Merith betrayed me."

"I don't understand," Galimar soothed with his words, slipping forward as his spoke.

"He betrayed us all when he destroyed the SolStone. When *you* destroyed the SolStone. Oberon knew that... wise Oberon. He knew Kaleus would become the greatest power. Kaleus would know how to use the SolStone as it should be used."

"And you want to help him." Galimar never took his eyes from Eron's face as he spoke — the wild-eyed face of a madman.

"Yes...I will be rewarded." Hatred seethed beneath his skin. "Never belittled...not like Merith. I could have controlled the SolStone. He never believed in me."

"You deserve so much better." Galimar held his breath and reached for the struggling bird.

"Noooo!" Eron screeched, pushing at the flailing bird.

It twisted in his hands, spinning backward, raking its claws down Galimar's forearms and hands. Eron fell backwards, turning, shoving the bird out the window but losing his balance at the same time. The Talec bird escaped, but he pulled Eron forward and out the stone window.

Eron clung frantically to the rock window ledge kicking at the night air. Galimar watched the Talec disappear into the black sky.

Reacting on instinct, Galimar dropped to his knees. He leaned forward with his head outside the window, over the sill that stood barely a hand's width high. He reached for Eron. Their hands connected immediately.

"I can't hold on." Eron whimpered.

Blood from the Talec's claw scratches dripped from Galimar's forearms slicking the fingers of his right hand. The hand that held Eron.

"You have to try!" Galimar ordered pulling with all his strength. "You can reach my other hand."

For the first time that evening, Eron truly saw Galimar. His anger was replaced with fear, and his vision cleared. He winced as he stared up into Galimar's uncovered face. The disfigured face that had been his friend. Ragged burns covered the left side of the Guardian's face. Slashing from his forehead, across his eyes, and onto his jaw.

"He did that to you?" Eron whispered.

At the shock of Galimar's wounds, Eron released his already slipping grip and fell.

"Nooo!" Galimar shrieked, clawing at the air as he watched his friend's body strike the castle wall and collapse to the ground below.

An insidious pain settled behind his jaw and twisted its way down his neck and into his back. Eron had been the spy. This man he had trusted, this man who knew all of his secrets, and now the Talec bird would carry Merith's plans to Oberon. The King, Richard, Keshar... everyone would be slaughtered in the crystal mines.

Jaika rushed to the floor beside Galimar. "I am going after them," Jaika reasoned. "They need to be warned. They've only been gone a while – we can catch them. You know the way. Two of us can ride faster. We won't have to hide the way they do. We are not a legion of men. We are only..."

"An old man and a girl," Galimar finished softly. "No one would suspect us."

"We have to find them before they get to the mines. Before they are..."

Galimar knew Merith would not want him to say yes, but he couldn't protect Jaika and warn his king. He could use a messenger, but who else might have worked with Eron? Who could he trust?

So with reluctance, he agreed. "Then we have to go now. There is not much time. They have almost a half a day ahead of us, but we can catch them. Can you ride?"

"Yes," Jaika lied. She had ridden a saktar following Richard and Davin, but they were moving slow and she had never really been in control. "I don't know," she said. "I don't know. I will try."

Galimar's cloak was gone and all of his scars were exposed. She could see the burns on his face and down his neck. They were on his hands, and she guessed they continued along his arm beneath his shirt sleeves. She did have memories of Galimar. Memories of him fighting... and her mother... her mother walking beside him. At least she thought it was her mother. Sometimes the images would mix together and she would see Richard and Inita in places she knew they could never have been.

"I will follow you," Jaika urged. "My father trusts you, and I trust you." She didn't want any of them to die. "Tell me what to do."

Galimar considered his options. It was two days across the desert. They would need supplies. "I have just the saktar for you. He is fast and jumps without looking, so you two should get along nicely."

Ride

The red moon was low but bright. There was little or no wind, and Galimar could see the print of the saktars that had gone before. He urged his mount to move faster. The prints in the sand were closer together, so they had been moving slow, trying to prevent a dust cloud that might be seen. But he... he and Jaika had to take that chance. A dust cloud would not matter now. The morning would bring the winds and the trail would disappear.

He kicked his saktar into a full gallop and watched Jaika cling to the saddle of her mount with a determination that had to be the part of Merith that lived within her. I will not fail her, he said to himself. We will not fail.

\#

Somewhere further along the sand, Merith slowed his men. He paused to study the moonlit sand, bringing his entire caravan to a halt. Beside him, the others scanned the dim horizon, not seeing anything of significance, just the sand, and the wind, and the moons, red and gold. They couldn't know that he searched for the ruins of a rock house. A three-room, rock house that had once been home to a warrior and a blue stone amulet, a SolStone that had changed his life forever.

The last soldier in the line of men saw them first. He sent the message up the ranks to Merith. Someone was coming. In the open desert, there was no place to hide, so they turned to face whoever rode so recklessly in the sand.

As they closed the distance, the soldiers recognized the scarred face of the mighty Galimar. He quickly explained the Talec and Eron and the inevitability of Kaleus's army. They agreed that their strategy must change, but it would take time to plan. They would continue their ride to the very edge of the Great Mountains where it was easy to find a make-shift cave in the rocks — a line of hopeful soldiers moving toward an insurmountable enemy. If anyone had cared to watch the travelers, they would never have guessed that one cloak covered a young woman and another a king.

#

Jaika's body ached from the night's ride and even the cold floor of a cave seemed welcoming her to sleep. She slid the saddle from her saktar and tied him at the entrance of the cave, weaving his straps around some loose rocks. The saddle left a winding trail in the sand as Jaika drug it deep into the shadows of the cave. Merith was already inside. He sat with his back to the rock wall staring at nothing. Jaika dropped her saddle and collapsed to the floor beside him waiting for him to speak, but he only stared, seeming not to see her or anything at all.

Jaika could feel the worries he carried so effortlessly and racked her brain to think of something brilliant to say. She so desperately wanted to know this man better.

"What were you praying for on the day we met?"

Merith jerked as though noticing her for the first time, then shot her a questioning look that quickly softened into a smile.

Jaika studied her father's face. His emotions were usually protected, but this time she had caught him off guard. This time her reward was a smile.

Merith shook his head and chuckled. "The first time we met you were a squirming, red faced kadel, and I prayed only that you would be born whole and safe."

Merith's eyes danced warm with the memories of Jaika's birth. The years seemed to melt from his face, and for an instant, he was that fearless young king calling Jaika to the shore of her dream river.

"That's not what I meant," she chided.

"I know," he relented and his youthful countenance faded. He studied his daughter's face, choosing his words. "Our kingdoms have been at war for so very long. So many men have died."

Merith brushed a wild wisp from Jaika's cheek. "Until that day...the day you came back to me...I had always prayed for victory. Victory over Kaleus." His voice rose. "I wanted the creator to help me destroy him."

"But on that day," Jaika prompted softly, afraid he would stop talking.

Merith drew a soulful breath of exhaustion. "On that day I prayed for guidance. I asked the creator to show me how to save my people."

"And he sent you a fiery scrap of a girl." Richard's interruption came out of nowhere. His boyish grin could be felt more than seen in the moonlit cave.

He knelt in front of Merith, his face heavy with admiration. "My Lord, my father wishes to speak with you."

"Of course." Merith's face clouded, his joy lost. "Will you stay with Jaika?"

His gentle words held a father's request as opposed

to his usual king's command.

"As long as she will have me," Richard answered, but he was looking at Jaika when he spoke, not at Merith.

Jaika tried not to read too much into those words.

Merith nodded and returned to his world of cold command, leaving behind his Jaika and their moment of happiness.

Richard stood before her in the darkness and listened to the fading footsteps. His sleek silhouette towered over her in the dim light.

"You should sleep now if you can."

He was not smiling now, she was sure.

"I will be close by."

His voice was strong and somehow she felt he would always be close by. She watched as he moved closer to the rocks and further away from her. Jaika tucked her cape around her body and leaned her head against the saktar's saddle.

She heard Richard settle against the rocks, shifting to find a comfortable spot to wait out the unbearable heat of the day. She could feel his eyes. Even without seeing, she knew he was watching her. He would always be watching out for her. Her body's desire for sleep was inescapable and she rested, peaceful, under his protective eye, dreaming of quiet waters.

The following night Richard and Keshar led the

small band of soldiers further along the rocky protection of the mountains. During the next day, again, they rested. But, the soldiers found only fitful sleep, dreaming about the cavernous mines and what lay inside, restless for the battle to begin. On the third night, their restlessness ended.

Camouflaged behind crumbling rocks, Keshar spotted two torches and four or five scattered glower pots outside the entrance to the mine shafts. Those living lights need a great deal of water and would truly be a luxury in this dry wasteland. In the yellow light he counted only two soldiers guarding the front entrance, and both wore the sleek, black uniforms of Kaleus's army.

The Captain motioned for his men to dismount and stay hidden. Each soldier slipped soundlessly from his saktar and secured his mount to the rocks. They moved as ghostly as any shadow and Jaika was amazed at their precision and complete lack of hesitation. Keshar had only to breath and his men bent to his will.

The Captain held up two fingers and motioned forward toward the other side of his rock hiding place. Richard edged his way backward in the line of soldiers until he found Jaika's side. He knew Merith would be close, but he wasn't taking any chances. When the battle started, he knew she would be killed just like any other soldier.

Pressing their bodies against the rocks, they tried

to remain as invisible as possible. Jaika's muscles tightened as she watched Keshar take down a guard with a quick slice of his blade. The other fell just as silently with a whisper of soldier's steel. A shiver pierced the back of her neck, and she turned away. She had no stomach for killing, no matter how necessary or deserved. Richard could taste her fear.

The other soldiers began disappearing in pairs around the edge of the rocks. She watched them cover the distance from their hiding place to the mine's entrance then disappear into the rock mountain. Richard slid his hand into Jaika's as their turn came, but she slipped from his grasp to lead the way — only fifty paces to the mine entrance.

"1, 2, 3...," she counted in her head, not knowing that Richard counted the same steps with soundless words.

Glowers lit the edges of the rocks and the entrance to the mine, illuminating the horrified expressions on the two dead guards. Jaika passed between their silent bodies and into the flickering torchlight of the mines. She tried desperately not to breath and not to brush against anything, especially anything dead. She knew if she dropped her focus for even a heartbeat she would cry out with the fear.

The glowers sent shadows dancing along the gray, stone walls of the mine — jagged, stone walls scarred by axes and explosives. Except for the faint, rhythmic clatter of metal, this place was like any other cave — dark, clammy, stale, and deathly cold. Jaika could feel the cold even in her bones.

Richard pressed next to her and kicked at a scampering kadel. Rats, thought Jaika, I never thought about rats in the mines. With a slimy twinge, she wondered what other unearthly animals might live within these rocks. She imagined slithering snakes and scorpions, then decided to let Richard take the lead.

With a quick motion to follow, Richard slunk down the rock hallway listening for Keshar and the others. Oberon knew they were coming. There should be more soldiers... somewhere. But, again, the only sounds were the distant metallic strokes, measured, even, mechanical strokes.

Edging deeper into the cave, they passed another stilled guard. Bloody evidence Keshar had left behind. As they traveled deeper in the mines, the rock gradually took on an iridescent quality. The walls began to shine like the walls of the castle. Jaika found herself wondering if the crystals would pass as diamonds on the other side of the SolStone gate. She would be a zillionaire in Mattie's city.

Two more guards lay in yet another stretch of the tunnel. Richard held up five fingers and made a slashing mark across his neck. Jaika understood all too well. Her plan had already cost five lives, and she knew there would be many more.

A few more steps and Richard jerked backward gripping Jaika's shoulder hard. She could feel him straining, listening. The metal clanking had stopped and the only sound was Richard's ragged breath. Jaika touched his hand to show she understood, then buried her fingers deep into his skin as a woman's scream echoed from the belly of the cave. A heavy clash of swords rang out, and both of them knew Keshar had been found.

Before Jaika could blink, Richard sprinted in the direction of the scream. Taking only a second to finish her gasp, the quivering princess followed fast on his heels. Somewhere along the way, Richard must have drawn his sword because he met the first soldier's advance without hesitation. He appeared as if pulled from a magician's hat — a black uniformed soldier of Kaleus's army. He dove at Richard from a turn in the rock, but he was not caught off guard. Three quick strokes and the attacking soldier fell. Jaika's heart sickened at the sight. Richard glanced in her direction to assure her safety, but he never faltered from the task at hand. His sword never slowed, and his face never lost the cold, emotionless look of a warrior.

Keshar barked orders around the next turn in the cavern, and Richard went immediately to find his father. Jaika's pace slowed, afraid of what she would find with the Captain of the Guard, but she followed anyway. Whatever lay ahead she certainly wasn't going to stay here alone.

The cavern wove in an 'S' pattern and she passed

two more dead guards before her eyes beheld Keshar and his soldiers. Four of Kaleus's men lay dead while only one of Merith's soldiers lay cold and still. Jaika did not even know his name, and her heart ached at the loss. She did not know any of these men. How many more would have to die?

Keshar's throaty voice shook at her fears. "The prisoners are kept further down the line. There may be more guards, so be prepared." In the flickering light Jaika could see the intensity in his eyes.

But, they found no more guards in the shadows...only tattered, faded workers. Pale skinned waifs chained every few feet along the rock walls. Sparkling, rich walls housing only despair and cruelty.

A young girl looked up at the passing soldiers with black, circled eyes. There was no joy or fear on her face — only exhaustion. She had no words to offer them.

Richard swung his sword and sent the first set of chains flying. A quiet gasp rippled along the line of people as they slowly realized what was happening.

"It's time to go home!" Richard shouted as he split another chain, and for the first time since their rescue began, Jaika saw traces of joy on his face.

The prisoner's desire for freedom was strong, but so was the fear ingrained in their hearts by their captors. Jaika expected them to run for the outside but instead they cowered in the hazy light of the cave.

Slowly a quiet procession began to move toward the entrance to the mine. Their faces numb and empty, still not sure they could truly believe in their own freedom.

Jaika wandered through the crowd unlocking shackles and inquiring of Mara. Torin said his wife had been in the mines for almost three years. Two long, horrible years in this dark, forgotten place. It was conceivable that she was already dead, but Jaika knew she had to try and find her. At least she would find the truth.

The princess fought the hollow ache in her body as the number of people grew. Tal, Sesti, Benjee... she had never seen so many different sects in one place. Kaleus did not care about the color of a person's skin. He did not care if you were man or woman or weak or strong. He would use anyone to find his crystals. A steady, unending stream of workers ebbed past her, holding out their arms as if they still wore chains. Many were too weak to ever attempt escape and their jailers had long since removed their restraints. Fear makes a powerful cage.

"Mara," Jaika whispered to the walking dead. "I seek Mara."

Word of her search must have spread because a young girl appeared out of the crowd motioning to Jaika. No more than ten, her once light hair matted with dirt and her eyes dull and dark. A tiny, frail echo of this dismal cave she called home. Perhaps it was the same girl

Jaika had seen when the chains were first being cut. Each face shared the same look of abandonment, and it was hard to tell them apart.

The child plodded forward swaying as she moved, as though the mere act of walking took her every ounce of strength. Jaika followed, terrified that the journey would end with a grave.

They moved toward the beginning of the mines. The deepest parts. The places with the most weathered of prisoners. Here the walls were heavy with trace crystal and there was no need for glowers.

"Mara," the young girl whispered, pointing to a crouching figure.

Jaika could see a tiny, malnourished woman not much bigger than the girl who had served as her guide. Her hair was black as night and her skin the ashen gray of the dead.

"Mara?" Jaika whispered kneeling beside the woman. "Are you Torin's Mara? Torin's wife?"

A tiny spark glimmered in the icy black of her eyes, but she did not answer.

"I want to take you to Torin." Jaika almost shouted at the woman.

"He's...dead..." she hissed just loud enough for Jaika to hear.

"He is alive and he misses you very much. Please

come with me."

Mara stared at Jaika wanting so much to believe, wanting so much to see Torin again. And then she nodded. Surely wherever this girl wanted her to go, it would be better than the mines. Anything was better than the mines.

Jaika lifted Mara from the ground as easily as a child and started toward the entrance. The nameless young girl followed with a soft glow of hope.

Richard reached out to take the woman as Jaika carried her through the crowds, but the princess shook her head. Mara wasn't heavy and Richard would need his sword arm free when more of Kaleus's soldiers appeared. He nodded in understanding...then jerked sideways. They had both heard it — gunfire. Toward the entrance of the mine. The battle for freedom was not over yet.

Richard ran toward the sounds. Jaika set Mara down and settled her behind a shadowy rock. "I will come back for you," she whispered, hoping that nothing would stop her from fulfilling her promise.

Drawing on the fear woven deep into her muscles, Jaika ran for the entrance of the cave. Her memory filled with the hours of training Davin and Richard had drilled into her flesh. Neither man could have foreseen just how their training would be tested. Dodging the prisoners that stood transfixed in her path, her body wove and shifted with practiced reflexes.

Jaika

The dusty tunnel stretched out before her. Flashes of gunfire splattered the walls in the turns of the shaft. Shadowy lightning bolts of gold streaking the rocks. She found herself counting the steps as she moved: 14, 15, 16... lifting her feet to eliminate even a whisper of a sound. A few steps toward the final turns at the entrance, Jaika flattened her body against the rocks, edging her way forward through the now silent cave.

She closed her eyes and listened to the space beyond. Her mouth tasting the musty air mixed with the burning ash of gunfire. She crept forward, watching for shadows, listening for a breath of a sound. Her feet moved silently in the dirt. Davin would have been pleased.

As her line of vision cleared the rocks, she saw three soldiers, motionless in the dirt. Two lifeless gray tunics of Merith's army. Jaika did not even know their names. A part of her died with them in that moment, and she knew a tiny fraction of what her father must always face.

Beyond the bodies, the space expanded and spread open at sharp angles. Black shadows trailed along the walls leaving a path wide enough to hide a single killer. Her eyes clawed at the darkness. If the killer made a sound, she would never have heard it over the drumbeats of her own heart.

Then one of the soldiers on the floor moaned. A low, pain-wracked groan, barely audible even in the silence. But it was enough. She saw the boot buckle in the shadows. A glimmer of metal from a man shifting his weight. She kept her eyes forward, away from the boot buckle, stifling the urge to help the soldier on the ground. She stepped forward, slowly, reaching toward the nearest body and his weapon. 1, 2, 3 steps forward. Before the forth step, she felt the bite of a rifle burn on her neck. A second shot and her knees buckled. She could see the black boots of a soldier step into the light and from behind her a laugh – an icy, cold, dark-hearted laugh. She felt strong fingers lace themselves into her hair as her body was jerked from the ground. Steel arms pulled her back against a black soldier's tunic. His chin pressing into her neck.

"I wondered where you went, my little Picari."

The heavy voice rumbled in her ear, and her heart sank. She knew the darkness in that voice all too well. She twisted in his arms and Oberon raised his gun to her head to quiet her struggle.

"Be still, my little one," he soothed. "I have been waiting for you."

He dragged her by the hair toward the entrance of the mine and out into the dawn. In the beginning rays of morning, Jaika could see soldiers scattered on the ground. Gray and black tuniced bodies mixed with blood so that they were impossible to count. And workers...faded, bloody, lifeless...scattered here and there. Oberon's men were killing the workers. And so, for the first time, Jaika saw the possibility of failure.

"Call to them," Oberon breathed in her ear. "Call to your father, to Richard. Bring them to me."

Jaika felt the warm blood running down her arm and neck from the gun burns. She closed her eyes and listened. It was too quiet. Her father, Richard, even the workers were hidden in the rocks and the shadows. She would never call them into the open. She would rather die.

Oberon slid his gun to the open wound on her neck and pushed. He drove the gun tip down into her flesh, and she screamed. Jaika grabbed at his arm, writhing with the pain.

In a heartbeat, Galimar appeared, facing Oberon across the sand. Oberon pulled the gun from Jaika's wound but kept it close to her head. Shaking it so Galimar would know that if he attacked, Jaika would die.

"Let her go," Galimar commanded, his voice calm as clear waters. "There is no reason for her to die."

"You can't save her." Oberon smiled. "Just like you couldn't save her mother."

Galimar swallowed hard and stepped closer. "Your soldiers are leaving you. Only a handful are left."

"She must fulfil the prophecy," Oberon's voice cracked.

Jaika could see Keshar and a handful of his

soldiers on the sand at the edge of the boulders. The sun's light exploding through the rocks to reveal their position.

"When the workers were released, the soldiers found their lost families. They will abandon you now." Galimar stepped closer. "They do not wish to serve a coward who hides behind a girl."

"I have the SolStone. I do not need soldiers. Once Jaika destroys Merith, I will be the greatest king. The full power of the SolStone will be mine and I will control all of Regar."

"The SolStone is difficult to use, isn't it." Galimar smiled, remembering all the nights he had spent trying to open the gateway. He had never truly unlocked all of the SolStone's powers.

Oberon's eyes grew wild with fury. "Merith is the lessor king. She will fulfil the prophecy!"

Jaika watched as the workers began reappearing out of the dusty light. They staggered back into the mines, passing her and Oberon as if they were not even there. *Why, why are you going back she wanted to scream. We let you out, why are you going back?*

Pft pft, a weapon fired in the distance. Beyond them someone screamed. Oberon's men were still killing the workers and forcing them back into the mines. Oberon yelled out a command that she did not understand. Four soldiers appeared out of the crowd in front of them, holding boxes, small boxes that glimmered in the light. Another command and the soldiers moved toward the mines.

"Butcher boxes," Galimar said under his breath. "You are going to explode the mines with the people inside? You need the crystals. Why would you destroy the mines?"

Oberon's vision cleared. "I don't need the crystals. Nothing matters but the prophecy. Merith must die. If you want to save your people, Merith must die."

"The prophecy is only words, Oberon." Galimar tried desperately to reach the man who had once served beside him. "It is only words. It does not dictate what you must do."

"She will fulfill the prophecy so that I may rule with the SolStone."

Merith stepped out of the shadows. He had been watching the scene play out before him, deciding what action to take. He wanted to save as many lives as possible.

He stepped toward Oberon. "Take my life, Oberon." Merith charged. "You have a weapon. Take my life!"

"No," Oberon slowly lowered his gun. "Jaika must do it, or I will destroy the mines. Every worker will die, and if they don't die they will be sealed in to starve. Maybe you will even hear their screams through the rubble."

The workers continued to fill the mines. There were very few on the outside now. Oberon pulled her backward, and turned her face to the entrance. She could see their faces looking out from behind the soldiers. Eyes from within the mines. A thousand eyes, weary eyes — hopeless and empty eyes.

"Take my life!" Merith screamed, holding his arms out, shoving his chest forward. "I am here! Destroy me!"

Oberon stepped back, releasing Jaika. "Take my weapon, my little Picari. Take my weapon and destroy your father — so that everyone in the mine will live."

"I don't believe you!" Jaika raged. "If I kill him, you will still destroy the mines. I don't believe anything you say!"

"Kill your father and I will let the workers go. If you deny me this, I will destroy everyone."

"No," came a voice from behind Merith. "My Mara, you will not kill her."

Suddenly Torin was there beside Galimar and Merith. Their bodies hazy in the morning light. Torin towered over the mighty Galimar.

Oberon shoved the gun into Jaika's hand forcing her to grip the weapon. "Destroy your father. Fulfill the prophecy."

"What if I kill you instead?" she said.

"Then the butcher boxes will be ignited." Oberon raised his voice to the sky. "Hear me my soldiers! If Merith does not die, destroy the mines!"

Jaika didn't know if the soldiers would follow his orders or not. She didn't know if they hated Merith or Oberon or why they were even there. She didn't want to kill her father. She didn't know what to do.

Jaika looked at Galimar. She looked at Torin and her father. It was all her fault. This was her plan. Why had it all gone so wrong?"

Screeeeeech!

Jaika heard the cries and then the wings. All eyes turned to see the heavy wings. Thousands upon thousands of Breen blocking out the sunlight. They filled the sky... and then they were everywhere. They were in her face and Oberon's face and the soldier's faces. They surrounded everyone, blocking out the light. She could feel their leathery wings pound against her skin. Their beaks ripping and tearing into the air. The deafening screeches of the Breen drowning all other sounds. Their eyes red as fire.

"No!" she screamed as they forced her backward. She dropped the weapon. She didn't mean to. It fell to the ground out of reach. She couldn't see it anymore. She couldn't see anything, just the wings. Thousands upon thousands of ebony wings.

Others began yelling too. Merith yelled...Galimar,

so many voices screaming. The Breen flailing in the darkness — the paralyzing darkness. Weapons firing and the cries of wounded Breen rose above the other sounds. Jaika could bare it no longer, and she fell to the ground and covered her face.

And then they were gone.

She could hear the wings as they rose above her. The sound of tents flapping in the breeze. Rising above her, disappearing. Their bodies dark against the sun. One Breen carried the lifeless body of a man. He hung by the waist — gripped by the talons of the Breen. Jaika thought she saw something dangling from his neck, but the sunlight made it difficult to be certain.

She stood to see the bodies on the ground. Bodies of the soldiers blocking the entrance to the mine. Four, five, maybe six new bodies. Soldiers the Breen had killed. She did not know who was dead and who was alive. Her heart ached at the sight.

Out of the chaos, Galimar lifted her from the ground. And she remembered... She remembered her mother and the sunlit day in the marketplace. She remembered Galimar and the yelling and the soldiers. She remembered her mother's screams as the soldiers took her, as they cut her to pieces. She remembered Galimar fighting, the fire, and the weapons. That horrible liquid that melted his flesh. She remembered all of it as he carried her out of the chaos.

"Help them, Gali," she cried. "Help the people.

Save them."

"They are already safe," he soothed. "The Breen saved them. The butcher boxes are gone. I don't know where Oberon is, but the people are safe. The soldiers will not fight. The people in the mine are safe."

Jaika could hear Torin's voice carried above the others. "Mara? Mara!" he screamed.

She knew he would find her. Somewhere in the cave, behind the shadowy rock.

#

It took days and wagons and saktars to take the people home. Oberon was lost. Jaika believed it was the Breen who took him, that limp body they carried through the sky. Still, everyone knew he would return one day. And, the SolStone would return with him. But for now, there was hope.

Galimar had not covered his face since the Breen's rescue. He worked tirelessly with the others to care for the mine workers and help find their families. It no longer mattered what sect each man claimed as his own or the color of a woman's skin. They were all children of Regar. They would all stand against Oberon when the time came.

But today, the sun was especially bright, and Galimar had found a red flower growing among the rocks.

"Richard tells me the Breen owed you a debt." The warrior bowed, just a little, and handed Jaika the tiny red flower. "Maybe someday you will tell me the story?"

Jaika nodded and smiled. "It's not as exciting as it sounds."

"Perhaps," Galimar scanned the horizon. "But still, the Breen were very brave. It is not an easy thing to pay a debt." He looked deep into Jaika's brown eyes. "I can never repay mine to you." He smiled at the flower, wrinkling his scars.

Jaika's brow creased a little as she looked at her friend. "I am afraid I don't understand."

Galimar studied the tiny, fiery girl in front of him. "You don't remember... your mother..." He touched the scars on his cheek as he spoke, seeing past events in his mind as clearly as the day they had taken place.

Jaika smiled. "I remember, Galimar."

The soldier winced at her words.

"I remember a day of shopping. Brightly colored tents, and flowers. An old lady with funny eyes gave me a flower, maybe like this one. She said it would bring me happiness."

Jaika moved closer to her friend, searching his eyes to find the past. "I remember soldiers in black. Angry soldiers on saktars riding through the market, with swords and chains. So many people fell, and there was so much blood. I remember an incredibly brave man standing between me and the soldiers, stopping one attacker and then another, swinging his sword until he could barely stand."

Then Jaika touched Galimar's face just below his eye. "I remember Kaleus throwing the fire crystals and you in front of me, your face burning as red as the fire that started in the tents. I remember dozens of men pulling you to the ground until you stopped moving."

Galimar shuddered and held back the angry tears. "But they killed your mother...I couldn't stop them."

"No one could, Gali," and she smiled up into his face. "I remember only your strength, your courage...your love. There is no debt to pay. There never was."

Galimar could not bring himself to speak, but his eyes held a thousand words. Love, gratitude, sorrow, he felt every moment of his past all at once. "You will make a fine queen someday, though not too soon I hope."

Jaika laughed. "If I am a fine queen it is only because I had such fine teachers."

In one motion, Galimar swept her into his arms, raising her from the ground to his lofty heights. Over his shoulder she could see her beloved Richard and her father already making plans. She knew she would be queen someday, but just as Galimar had said, she hoped it would be a long time in the future.

 And Richard... he would make a fine king.

FREE BONUS CHAPTER

Visit my website

https://alexraebooks.wordpress.com/

to explore other books in the **Children of Regar** series and to receive a

FREE BONUS CHAPTER

I would love to hear from you:
Watch for upcoming stories on
Facebook @AlexRaeBooks
or email me at AlexRaeBooks@gmail.com